The Recruiting Trip

The University of Gatica Series, Volume 1

Lexy Timms

Published by Dark Shadow Publishing, 2014.

The Recruiting Trip
By
Lexy Timms
Copyright 2014 by Lexy Timms

All rights reserved. No part of this publication may be reproduced, stored in or introduced into a retrieval system, or transmitted, in any form, or by any means (electronic, mechanical, photocopying, recording, or otherwise) without the prior written permission of both the copyright owner and the above publisher of this book.

This is a work of fiction. Names, characters, places, brands, media, and incidents are either the product of the author's imagination or are used fictitiously. Any resemblance to an actual person, living or dead, events, or locales is entirely coincidental. The author acknowledges the trademarked status and trademark owners of various products referenced in this work of fiction, which have been used without permission. The publication/use of these trademarks is not authorized, associated with, or sponsored by the trademark owners.

All rights reserved.
Copyright 2014 by Lexy Timms
Cover design by: Book Cover by Design
No part of this book may be used or reproduced in any manner whatsoever without written permission, except in the case of brief quotations embodied in articles and reviews.

Also by Lexy Timms

Saving Forever
Saving Forever - Part 1
Saving Forever - Part 2
Saving Forever - Part 3
Saving Forever - Part 4

The University of Gatica Series
The Recruiting Trip

Standalone
Wash
Loving Charity
Summer Lovin'
Christmas Magic: A Romance Anthology

Website: https://www.facebook.com/SavingForever
Book Trailer:
http://www.youtube.com/watch?v=5FdSZUaJ2q0

UNIVERITY OF GATICA SERIES
The Recruiting Trip
Book One is now available!
Faster
Book Two: Coming January 2015

This is Book 1 of a 4 book series
DESCRIPTION:

Aspiring college athlete Aileen Nessa is finding the recruiting process beyond daunting. Being ranked #10 in the world for the 100m hurdles at the age of eighteen is not a fluke, even though she believes that one race, where everything clinked magically together, might be. American universities don't seem to think so. Letters are pouring in from all over the country.

As she faces the challenge of differentiating between a college's genuine commitment to her or just empty promises from talent-seeking coaches, Aileen heads to Gatica State University, a Division One school, on a recruiting trip.

THE RECRUITING TRIP 3

The university's athletic program boasts one of the top sprint coaches in the country. The beautiful old buildings on campus and Ivy League smarts seems so above her little Ohio town upbringing. All Aileen needs to convince her to sign her letter of intent is a recruiting trip that takes her breath away.

Tyrone Jensen is the school's NCAA champion in the hurdles and Jim Thorpe recipient for top defensive back in football. His incredible ocean blue eyes and confident smile make Aileen stutter and forget why she is visiting GSU. His offer to take her under his wing, should she choose to come to Gatica, is a temping proposition that has her wondering if she might be making a deal with an angel or the devil himself.

* This is NOT erotica* It is a new adult & college sport romance.

For mature readers only. There are sexual situations, but no graphic sex.

UNIVERSITY of GATICA SERIES
The Recruiting Trip
Faster
Higher
Stronger

THE RECRUITING TRIP

Citius, Altius, Fortius

Prologue

From: Coach Anderson (C.Anderson@gatica.edu)
Date: Sat, November 1, 2015 at 12:34PM EST
Subject: GO REDCOATS!
To: Aileen Nessa (hurdlesrock@gmail.com)
Hi Aileen,

I am so excited to contact you again. Since we last spoke in September, I have been looking forward to this chance to get to know more about you. You're an amazing athlete, extremely talented and fun to watch. You have a great attitude, work ethic and passion for our sport. I know you would be a great fit with our program. I hope you know how excited I am about you as a potential student-athlete at University of Gatica.

I know you are getting tons of pressure from other universities, most of which want an early verbal commitment but I hope you hang in there with us and that you give yourself the time you need to make the best possible decision for yourself. I believe you have the talent and ability to not only gain admission to Gatica, but be a future leader in our program and an impact performer on our team.

As we discussed early in September, the best weekend for an unofficial visit to campus would be February 10-12. We are hosting an indoor meet that weekend and would love it if you had a chance to see the Red Coats in action. Of course, if that doesn't work we will host you any time that's convenient for you.

Coach Maves, the sprint coach will be communicating with you regularly via email to share information about Gatica. If you have any questions or would like to chat, I am always available by email or phone.

I look forward to hearing from you soon.
Best wishes,
Coach Anderson
Coach Anderson
Head Coach, Woman + Men's Track and Field
c.anderson@gatica.edu

Chapter 1

"Aileen... N-Nessa?"

She nodded as she swung her back pack over her shoulder. "That's me." A guy jostled past her mumbling something about baggage claim sucking.

The chauffer driver tucked the sign with her name printed on it under his arm and took her small carryon suitcase. "First time coming to Gatica?"

"It is." She glanced around the airport wondering why one of the coaches at the University of Gatica hadn't come to greet her. It seemed weird. Sort of. She had no idea what proper protocol was. Were coaches required to meet recruits when they arrived? Or was a shuttle service completely legit?

She had been on four other recruiting trips, the last on two months ago in Miami. The sprint coach there had picked her up from the airport, but the university was about fifteen minutes away from the school.

The chauffer led her outside. She dug through her bag and slipped her sunglasses on against the bright sun.

"You here on a recruiting trip?" The chauffer glanced at her. "Volleyball?"

She shook her head. "Track."

"Cool." He loaded the 'UofG Travellers' van. "The memo says to drop you off Wavertree Fieldhouse. It holds the indoor track and the girls' volleyball gym. They have a gym off the track and then a court set up in the middle of the track for games. It's pretty impressive to watch a game courtside or up in the bleachers above the track."

Aileen nodded, pretending to be interested. She couldn't picture what he meant. Her indoor track was a gym at the high school. Basketball, volleyball, badminton or whatever sport was going on at the time shared the gym with her. Her coach happened to be her high school gym teacher and he was awesome. He wanted her to go to Connecticut or Louisiana, somewhere with a strong woman's track program. She agreed.

UofG had been a last minute choice for her final recruiting trip because of their near Ivy League status – and the fact that the super-hot looking male NCAA champion happened to attend the school.

Aileen's best friend, Becky, had dared her to go. She had gone through all the brochures at Aileen's house and said she needed to go on one recruiting trip based on something other than track. Becky had insisted UofG because of the hot guys. Aileen had said yes because of Tyler Jensen.

She had watched him race at the USTAF championships last summer. He had this amazing physique, all muscle with no fat and a six pack which really should be referred to as a twelve pack. However it wasn't his body that always had her staring at him, it was his face. The short, perfectly cropped hair against his naturally tanned skin and those unbelievable eyes.

She had picked UofG in the hopes of talking to him close up just so she could figure out what his eye color really was.

It was ridiculous. Stupid. She knew it, but nobody knew the real reason she had come to Gatica except Becky, and she only knew half of it. Aileen had never voiced her silly crush out loud. Nobody knew, and she planned to keep it that way.

"Ms Nessa?" The grandfather aged chauffeur lifted his foot off the gas. "Are you alright?"

She tuned back into the present and realized they were on the highway. "Sorry, pardon?"

"I was just wondering if you needed a drink? We've got about an hour and a half before we reach Gatica. Do you need anything?"

"No thanks. I've got a bottle of water here." She could feel the heat in her cheeks but refused to acknowledge it. She stuffed her ear buds in and turned her iPod on, hoping it would defer monsieur chauffeur from chatting.

It didn't work.

"So, where are you from?"

She paused hoping he would think she couldn't hear him. When he repeated the question louder, she imagined her mother sitting beside her giving her *the* look. "From Ohio. Bucyrus."

"What event do you do?"

"Hurdles."

"Sprint or four hundred?"

"Sprint."

"Are you any good?"

Aileen shrugged. "Pretty good for high school. Not so sure about university level." She had spent the past year and half comparing her times to NCAA students. If she compared her personal best to last year's outdoor rankings she would be second. Her indoor times this year weren't so great, only because her coach wanted to focus on the upcoming summer and trying to make the World Junior Championships. However she wasn't going to brag to a total stranger. She had to believe in herself, not make other people believe.

"Well you've got five years to find out." His walkie talkie two-way radio buzzed and a woman's voice came through the line. Mr. Chauffeur replied.

Aileen leaned back against the bench and closed her eyes. Her flight had been early this morning. She was tired but could never sleep while travelling. She went over her high school coach's instructions for training. They usually planned a hard workout for Fridays so she could take Saturday easy.

He hadn't been impressed with her decision to use her last recruiting trip on UofG and made today's workout tougher than usual. When she moaned about it, his only sympathy came by saying she could do the workout Saturday instead. She still had to do it.

It sucked having to call the coach here in Gatica the day before she left and ask if she would be able to use the weight room and possibly the track. At least Coach Anderson had been totally understanding and said it wouldn't be a problem. With the track meet tomorrow she could use it today or possibly early tomorrow morning.

Guess it all depended on what she would be doing on the trip. She didn't think tonight would be late. The athletes had their meet tomorrow. Doing the workout in the morning seemed easier than trying to squeeze it in today. Coach Anderson had mentioned a campus tour today before practice at three o'clock.

She peeked at her watch. If the chauffeur drove at least the speed limit, they would arrive just before lunch.

"Did you know we have a good hurdler here already?" The chauffeur turned the radio down and looked at her in the review mirror.

Aileen blinked and ran the question over in her head. She thought she knew who all the hurdlers were. Gatica had a good multi eventer who could hurdle, but no strong female sprint hurdlers. "Who?"

"Tyler Jensen." He nodded. "That boy's extremely talented. Athletically, and I read in the paper the other day he's up for making the dean's list in academics. He's taking some kind of sport major."

She nodded. She knew exactly who Tyler Jensen was. His beautiful, chiselled face graced the cover of the track brochure and his long, muscular body hovered over a hurdle on the inside. He had these amazing coloured eyes. They looked green, or blue, or grey. She couldn't decide from the picture or from the times she had watched him race this summer.

They had both competed at nationals. She was a nobody junior and he the NCAA champion. She had watched all his races at nationals and felt his disappointment when he finished fourth in the finals. It was a good, clean race until the last hurdle when he stumbled slightly and lost a placing from it. Third would have meant a trip to the World Championships.

She didn't even make the finals. She came ninth, one place away from the finals. Last summer she turned eighteen while at nationals. Her mom and dad had come to watch her race and taken her out for ice cream afterwards. She hadn't cared, two weeks before she had placed fourth at junior nationals and missed making the Can-Am international meet.

Tyler was over nineteen so he hadn't competed at the junior nationals. It wasn't until the meet in California she had noticed how cute he was. He had the perfect tan, the kind of skin that never faded in the winter. His dark hair was cropped short. It all brought out those eyes. You could notice them from the finish line, a hundred and ten meters away from where he stood before his starting blocks.

They had never spoken to each other. She ran one more race last season and blew everyone away, beating the national champion and world bronze medalist. Her time was a hundredth off the American junior record and the tenth fastest time in the world that summer.

Now she had every school in the country recruiting her, sending brochures, letters and phone calls every night. She had gone on four trips and picked Gatica as her last trip.

"Have you ever seen Tyler race?"

Aileen smiled and leaned forward in her seat. She didn't mind talking about Tyler Jensen. She just couldn't refer to him as Tyler... yet. "I watched him this summer at nationals. He just missed out on a medal."

The driver nodded. "He was probably burnt out. Between football and then winning NCAAs in track, he probably had nothing left in the tank by the end of July."

"Good point. " She hadn't thought about that. She knew he played football because the brochure boasted about some medal or award he had won. She wasn't a football fanatic. Her cousin said it would all change when she started university and got into college football. She highly doubted it, except if she was here in Gatica, then she would watch every game. It wasn't going to happen though. She had pretty much told Stanford she would be there in September.

"So you've never been to Gatica?"

She shook her head. "I've only been to New York once. My parents and I went on holiday to Niagara Falls one time."

"Niagara Falls is nice. It's about three hours from here."

He chatted on about other great places to see in New York and the restaurants she needed to try while in Gatica. Before long he was pulling the van off the highway.

"We're about ten minutes from the school. I'll drop you off right in front of Wavertree Fieldhouse. The track offices are to the right of the main entrance on the first floor. You'll have no problem finding them."

Butterflies began wiping around in Aileen's stomach. She pulled her make-up bag out of her backpack and slipped on some lip gloss and then deodorant when the drive wasn't looking. She hoped her hair looked okay. She had straightened it last night and then stuck it in a ponytail this morning. The pony had come out a few times as she tried to keep it straight and neat. Her blonde hair preferred to have a mind of its own so she usually lived with a pony and hairband to keep the frizzy's in check.

Forest trees cut away to houses. Total college town.

"I'll take you through Campus Corner."

"Campus Corner?" Aileen tried to remember if she had read about it and couldn't recall.

"It's the strip where the college kids hang out. Restaurants, shops, bars, all the things you kids need for a proper college experience." He chuckled. "If you live on this side of campus, it's walking distance."

He turned the van left and then right.

Aileen looked out the window. Little shops and restaurants had the Gatica symbol. An old movie theater had been renovated into a bar named "The Red Coats" and had an army of soldiers painted on the front of the building.

"That's where all the sport kids hang out." The driver told her about other places and when he came to a stop sign he pointed to his right. "Here's the entrance to U of G. It's the original signed from eighteen seventy-six. They've repainted the soldier but the horse and soldier monument where erected when the school opened."

A larger than life monument stood beside a stone with University of Gatica 1876 engraved in it. The monument was made of brass or copper or something that had turned green over time but the soldier's coat and hat were painted a bright, poppy red.

Aileen smiled. It was awesome!

The campus was built out of the same stone as the plaque at the front. Maybe limestone or something like that. The buildings each had vintage character to them but with a twist of the twenty-first century. She imagined walking around the campus in fall would be amazing. Even the light layer of snow covering the ground now added to the picturesque seen.

They drove by the outdoor track stadium. Someone had shovelled the two inside lanes and the mondo red track stood out bright against the snow. Behind the track was a building that looked like something that held airplanes. It had to be the indoor track – Wavertree Fieldhouse.

Aileen zipped up her coat and took a deep breath as the van pulled around and stopped in front of the building.

THE RECRUITING TRIP 15

Here we go.

Chapter 2

A cold wind picked up and whipped Aileen's pony to the side, slapping it against her cheek. She shut her eyes so the ends of her hair wouldn't poke her eyes. Blinking, she refocused as she pulled her pony and then threw her hood on to stop it from swinging.

The driver set her suitcase beside her. "Can you sign this so they know I dropped you off in the right spot?" He handed her his clip board and a pen.

The pen didn't want to write. She shook it and finally got the ink to flow so she could sign her name.

"Have a good trip." He jumped in his SUV and drove away, leaving Aileen standing in the cold in front of the building.

A girl wearing a bright red coat came out of the building and jogged down the steps. She paused by Aileen as she put her knit cap on.

"Hi." Aileen stood staring at the girl, the least she could do was say hello.

"Hey." She smiled. Her dark brown hair disappeared inside her hat. Her smiled reached her pretty brown eyes. "Are you the hurdler?"

"I think so."

"You here on a recruiting trip?"

"Yup." Aileen felt silly holding the handle of her suitcase and shaking because of the cold. Ohio was cold, but this was freezing!

"Come on. I'll take you to Coach Anderson." She turned and jogged up the large cement steps to the door she had just come out of. She held the door open for Aileen. "I'm Jani, by the way."

"I'm Aileen."

"Cool. Where are you from?"

"Bucyrus, Ohio." She set her suitcase down and pulled the handle out again to drag it by its wheels. "Where are you from?"

"Canada. B.C. West Coast. Mountain country." She laughed when Aileen nodded, as if it made sense why she didn't seem to have issue with the cold weather. "I may be from Canada, but it doesn't get this bloomin' cold where I live. I had to go and buy another tuque last night. I keep leaving mine at track or where ever and people are nipping them."

"Tuque?"

Jani pointed to her hat. "Tuque. Canadian hat." She laughed. She had a contagious kind of laugh that made Aileen smile. "I keep telling Coach he needs to slap a Red Coat on the front and sell them for money for the program."

"It sounds like a good idea." Aileen walked beside Jani, noticing how short she was compared to the friendly, chatty girl. "Do you play volleyball?" The girl was tall and Aileen vaguely remembered that the chauffeur had mentioned the volleyball team trained there as well.

"I'm a high jumper." She elbowed Aileen and leaned in. "Not saying I haven't chatted up the cute volleyball assistant coach. He's working on his master's degree and coaching part time. Super hot."

Aileen nodded, not sure how to respond. *Maybe a little too much information?*

Jani giggled again. "The volleyball offices are just down the hall from the track office. Wavertree is back there." She pointed behind them. "You go left where we came in. It'll take you to the indoor track."

They passed a trophy case with old track and field equipment inside it, along with black and white photos.

Jani tapped the case. "These things are all over the place. The original ones start here and as you make your way down to the indoor track they move up to present day. It's kinda neat." She slowed and opened a door with frosted class.

On the glass was written Athletics T&F. A plaque below the glass showed Coach Anderson as the head coach. The jumps coach, distance coach and whoever else was listed as well, but Aileen didn't get a chance to read all the names because Jani leaned against the door to let her in.

The scent of new runners waffled through the door. Aileen unzipped her jacket and pulled her hat off. The heat from the office felt ten degrees warmer than it probably was.

A small desk sat directly in front of the door. A petite lady, a few years older than her mom, smiled at the two of them. She pushed her chair back and stood up. "Jani! Did you forget something?"

"I found this poor recruit freezing her butt off outside. Is Coach Anderson still in his office?" Jani winked at Aileen. "This is Marge. She's the track secretary and totally awesome. She keeps Coach Anderson in line."

Marge smiled and came around her desk with a file folder. "Aileen Nessa, right?"

She held out her hand, but Marge gave her a hug, surprising Aileen.

"I printed off an itinerary for the weekend." Marge opened the folder. "Coach Anderson mentioned you would need to train so just look over the schedule and let me know if you need a ride to the track."

Her face was open, her expression genuine; she seemed really sweet. Aileen looked over the schedule. "Probably tomorrow morning before the track meet. I'm supposed to lift weights. Is there a weight room here at the track?"

Jani shook her head. "We lift at the football stadium. There is a little weight room here but it stinks. Only the distance runners use it so there aren't any weights heavier than ten pounds." She nudged Aileen. "Way better view at the football stadium anyway. Most of the varsity athletes lift there."

Jani sounded like Becky. *All about boys. Both of them.*

Marge cleared her throat. "Just tell me what time you want to work out and I'll make sure you have a ride to the weight room. The track meet starts at ten. The Holiday Inn you are staying at includes breakfast. If you don't mind taking care of your own breakfast tomorrow, Coach Anderson will take you out on Sunday morning so you two can chat."

"Okay. Sounds good." Aileen dropped her backpack off her shoulder and stuffed the schedule inside.

Jani grabbed her suitcase and tucked it next to a filing cabinet beside the door. "Let's go meet the coach." She grabbed Aileen's hand and led the way.

There were three offices to the left of Marge's desk and then a pair of French doors with frosted glass. Jani knocked on one of the doors and poked her head through the small opening. "Coach?"

"Jani!" A husky voice called out.

Jani opened the door all the way. "Aileen's here."

The large office was easily the space of the three offices on the other side. A beautiful oak desk sat in the middle of the room surrounded by photos and plaques all over the wall. A large photo of Tyler Jensen hung on one side. It was black and white except for the burgundy red uniform. Aileen glanced at the other pictures and then over to the Coach.

Coach Anderson sat behind the laptop on his desk. He wore a dress shirt, and Aileen guessed there was probably a suit jacket hanging on the back of his chair. He was in his fifties with a dusting of gray hair and bright blue eyes. He smiled when their eyes met, and stood up.

"It's great to finally meet you, Aileen." He came around the desk and held out his hand.

She returned the firm handshake.

"Jani, thanks for bringing Aileen in."

"No problem." Jani checked her watch. "I've got to jet. I'm going to be late for class." She smiled at Aileen. "I'll see you at practice later. Coach Anderson asked me to take you out for dinner tomorrow night after the meet. We'll catch a movie or something after." She turned slightly so the coach wouldn't see her wink. "We'll figure something out. See ya." She saluted Coach Anderson before leaving.

Coach Anderson chuckled before pointed to a leather chair for Aileen to sit down in. He went back around the desk. "Jani's a fireball. She's got lots of spirit. You won't be bored around her." His phone began to ring. He checked the caller ID before muting it. "Jani broke the school high jump record as a freshman last year. She qualified for NCAA's indoor and outdoor last year. Coach Maves is the jumps coach. She thinks Jani will set a new PR at tomorrow's meet." He leaned back, resting his elbows on the arms of his chair, and folding his hands together. "I'd like to hear about you. How is school going? Training?"

Aileen was used to this. The past four recruiting trips had all the coaches asking her the same questions. "School's good."

"By your GPA, it looks like you aren't having any problems." Coach Anderson chuckled. "Do you know what you want to study when you start university?" He scratched his jawline. "Last time we talked you said you weren't sure."

"I'm still trying to decide. I like the sciences. Maybe biology or something like that."

"Gatica has a very strong science department. If you decide to major in biology, or any life science jobs, it opens you up to a lot of possibilities like biotechnology, pharmaceutical, post doctorate. We have a fantastic master's program here as well. There is also kinesiology. A lot of the athletes at the school get into the kin or physio therapy program. The school just added a new sport therapy program to go with it. The classes filled very quickly."

"I'll have to look into the program." She said politely. They did interest her, more than dissecting frogs and rats for the next four years. She just wasn't sure she wanted to show any interest in anything particular.

"And how's training going?"

She didn't mean to, but a sigh slipped from her lips. "It's going. My high school coach has me training through indoors to focus junior nationals this summer."

Coach Anderson nodded. "It's not a bad idea. I know it's more fun to compete than it is to train, but it'll pay off in the long run."

She nodded, glad he got it. "I like training. It's fun practicing or doing plyometrics and stuff in the weight room. My coach just has some crazy ideas for combining weight room stuff with plyos. Since I'm from a small town and we only train at the high school, he likes finding things in the school to use for training." She laughed. "Last week he decided to make an obstacle course inside the school. I mean down the halls. He found this old tire and filled half of it with sand and made me run stairs with it, then drop it and hop over these old chairs he had found in a storage room. I had to hurdle them! It was crazy. They were set so the chair part was facing me and I have to get my lead leg down fast or I'd nail the next chair. It was deadly." She still had a good bruise on her shin to prove it.

"I think I like your coach." Coach Anderson smiled. "I like his work ethic. We just happened to have a better choice of training equipment to use. Gatica's football program had a state of the art weight room and training facility that all the varsity sports use. You'll see it tomorrow morning." He pointed to a panoramic picture hanging beside Tyler Jensen's picture. It showed the indoor track. "We have cold winters. I won't lie to you about that. However our indoor facility has hosted Indoor Nationals and international meets. It's one of the best in the country. We do warm weather training over spring break, usually down in Florida, and also head south for a number of our opening outdoor meets of the season. It works well for us."

She liked the idea of spending a weekend in Florida, especially if the cold weather ran into March or longer. Stanford, on the other hand, was warm all year long.

His phone began vibrating. He checked the call. "Shoot! I have to take this." He shot her an apologetic smile and then glanced behind her. "Coach Maves!"

Aileen turned in her chair to see the jumps coach. Coach Maves looked a few years younger than Coach Anderson. She was about five foot seven, close to the same height as Aileen and had short dirty blonde hair kept in check by a simple headband.

She smiled at Aileen. "Perfect timing. I was about to ask if you were ready for lunch?"

"Sure." Aileen stood and slipped her backpack over her shoulder. She looked at Coach Anderson who had picked up his phone. He moved it away from his mouth so he could speak to her. "Maves will take you to lunch. I'll see you again at practice?"

She nodded. It sounded good to her. She followed Maves out of the office and paused by the track office main door. "Should I take my suitcase?"

Maves paused. "I'll toss it in my office while we are out." She picked up the suitcase and set it in her office. She grabbed a file off her desk. "You have... a campus tour after lunch. I'll keep the case in here and you can grab it after the tour. If there's time between the tour and practice, I can take you to the hotel to check in. Otherwise one of us will drop you off after." She slipped her coat on and wrapped a scarf around her neck. "You hungry?"

Aileen checked her watch. It was just after one. "Yeah," she admitted honestly.

"Then how about we hit the Student Union? It's a short walk and we can cut through the field house." She led the way out of the office and waited for Aileen in the hall.

Aileen followed her and they headed down the hall where she had come in, and then off to where Jani had pointed to earlier.

THE RECRUITING TRIP

"The school mascot is a red coat soldier. The school color was originally a poppy red. Over the years the color has changed to more of a burgundy color. The track uniforms are burgundy red while the football team still uses the poppy red color. We changed ours about two years ago." She chuckled. "The team kept complaining the poppy red was bleeding into their other clothes. Apparently a lot of the track team doesn't know how to separate their whites from their darks."

Aileen nodded but had no idea what she meant. She'd never done a load of laundry in her life. She guessed she would be asking her mom to teach her this summer.

They came to a T-section in the hall. Maves pointed to the left. "That'll take you to showers and change rooms. The other way heads down to Kinesiology and sport classes, and also our medic rooms. We have a room set for massage therapy, where a number of the athletes receive a massage once a week, and possibly more if needed. There is a large rehab room that we share with the volleyball team. There are ice baths, ultrasound, physio and whatever else you need. We baseline test two times a year and they help out with BMI, body fat percentage... all that kind of jazz."

She started walking forward again. "This will lead you outside and also to the indoor track." She pulled on a large set of metal doors.

The ground changed from grey tile to reddish pink mondo track beyond the door. Aileen stepped through the door held open for her and peered around. The pictures on the brochure and school website had showed the track, but the reality of it obviously couldn't be captured in pictures. It was huge and awe-inspiring.

Her heart rate sped and she glanced up at the large stained glass windows and seats that surrounded the track, above them. One of the large windows had a red coat soldier depicted on it. The place was amazing.

"Art students have painted the lead glass over the years. It's pretty neat."

"It is." Aileen was at a loss for words. The empty track contained six lanes. Hurdles were set measured perfectly on one of the straightaways. The high jump mats were on the far side and pole vault mats were just across from her. She had the itch to settle into one of the starting blocks and race to the first hurdle. She inhaled slowly, taking in the scent of rubber, sweat and cool air.

She could stay here forever.

"If we cut across, there are entrances we can use. They are open on the inside but locked outside... unless there's a meet or a volleyball game. They have the same painted lead glass on them too." Coach Maves started across the track.

Aileen hesitated to cut across. This was sacred ground on pretty much any track. You never cut across, you always walked around. At least that's what she believed. Yet, here she was, falling behind because she hesitated to break the rules? She grinned and jogged to catch up to Coach Maves.

What fun was following the rules anyway?

Chapter 3

Outside, Aileen zipped up her jacket once again, and slipped its hood over her head. She stuffed her hands deep into her pockets and walked beside Coach Maves.

"The Student Union is a crazy hub of activity," Maves commented. "It has just about everything, from student council activities, to study rooms; the cafeteria and also a pub with pool tables, darts, and other games are set up on the lower floor."

A blast of warm air hit them as they walked inside, along with somebody dressed in a red coat; sporting a blow up horse they were pretending to ride.

Aileen burst out laughing as she flipped her hood back. The guy was carrying a water gun but it must have broken. The one side of his jacket was drenched and the gun seemed to only sputter a few drips.

"Beware fair maiden," he shouted at her. "I will protect you." He stepped between her and Coach Maves, pulling out a plastic sword and swinging it in the coach's direction. "Ol' Maves, I know about your treachery."

"Sean McFarland! If you hit me with that thing you are going to be running outside for practice!" Maves grabbed at the plastic sword just as Sean jumped back and crashed into Aileen.

She lost her balance and fell to the ground. A huge POP! sounded as Sean tumbled and landed on top of her. "Oh no!"

"My horse! My horse!" Sean scrambled up and lifted his deflating horse's head. He spun around to help Aileen. "Are you alright?" He held his hand out to pull her up.

"I'm fine." Surprisingly she was. When he had fallen on top of her, she'd expected to get the wind knocked out of her lungs.

Instead, it had felt more like a heavy, bony blanket. The guy couldn't have weighed more than a hundred and ten pounds. *Distance runner.*

Coach Maves grabbed Sean's sword and bopped him on the head with it. "Sean, this is Aileen. She's visiting from Ohio."

Sean pulled his funny looking hat off, revealing a dusty brown mop of hair. He had cute freckles sprinkled across the bridge of his nose and bright blue eyes.

"Sean is a freshman. He's running the mile tomorrow."

Sean grinned at Aileen. "What event do you do?"

"Hurdles."

"Cool." He shot a glance at Maves and smiled as he winked at her. "You taking good care of Aileen, Coach Maves? If you want, I can take her off your hands and show her the school. I've got nothing till practice."

"No classes?" Maves frowned. "That's a lot of free time for a freshman."

"Just Friday's, Ma'am. I set the schedule to work with indoor and outdoor season this semester."

Maves nodded, but it didn't look like she believed him. "I'm taking her to lunch now but if she wants, you can show her around campus after." She crossed her arms over her chest. "You need to get out of that ridiculous outfit first though."

Aileen pressed her lips tight together to supress a laugh. She could tell Coach Maves was trying to do the same.

Sean pumped his fist in the air. "Meet you back here in thirty minutes!" He hugged Maves. "I know you love me. I'll give her the best campus tour ever!" He ran out the doors, spun around outside and came back in. "Forgot my backpack." He raced off in the other direction.

They watched him dash around and through people scattered throughout the place.

"Is he always..." Aileen let her voice trail off. She wasn't sure what to say. Hyper? Spastic? Crazy?

"Pretty much." Maves chuckled. "He's a good kid. His heart's in the right place and he's a decent runner. Slightly on the crazy side, but there's never a dull moment when he's around." She began walking through the busy hallway and then stopped for a moment. " It's just occurred to me that I didn't ask you if you wanted to go off with him? I'm sorry, I should have asked. It's hard not to get caught up with silly Sean."

"Sean seems great. I don't mind. I'll go with him." She was pretty sure Sean's version of the campus visit would be a whole lot funnier than a proper drawn out one. Also, at least with Sean, Aileen could say she'd seen enough if she was getting cold. He could just show her the interesting buildings and skip all the boring stuff.

Maves pulled out her phone and began texting. "I'll let Coach Anderson know. What do you feel like for lunch?"

They headed into the cafeteria, ordered lunch and settled at a table.

"Are you enjoying your senior year of high school?" Maves asked.

Aileen finished a bite of her sub. "It's going by so fast. Becky, she's my best friend, keeps saying graduation is going to be here before you know it."

"Does Becky run track?"

Aileen shook her head and giggled. "Not unless she's running to a store to grab a new song track. Becky's into music, big time. Sports, not so much." She thought about Becky. They had been best buds since first grade. Would college change things between them?

"Does Becky have plans for after graduation?"

"She's in this band. They're really good, actually." Aileen pointed to her backpack. "I have them on my iPod. Beck's already been accepted to the University of Ohio. She's going to major in music. One of the guys in the band enrolled as well and the other two are going with them so they can keep playing together." She had realized after last summer there was no way they would be going to university together. It sucked, but they had promised each other it would work out. They would never lose touch and be best buds forever, maids of honour at each other's weddings, godmothers to their kids, etc... They had it all planned out.

"She sounds interesting."

Interesting was definitely not the word she would have used to describe Becky. Aileen laughed. "She's crazy."

"Like Sean-crazy?" Maves raised an eyebrow.

"Probably close." Aileen grinned. She liked Maves.

"Then she will be the best and strongest of friends who will never let you down."

Aileen turned around to see who had spoken the words.

Sean stood, arms crossed, now dressed in a pair of jeans and UofG track sweatshirt. He shrugged and looked back and forth between the two of them. "Don't look so surprised. Crazy people are beyond loyal."

Maves gave a disbelieving nod. "Don't scare her, Sean. The purpose of a recruiting trip is to convince an athlete this is the place for them. Not have them running for the hills as fast as they can."

"Does he always spout prophecies?"

"Sometimes," Maves said. "The odd time just before a cross country race and I think I've heard him once or twice this indoor season."

"Why kind of things does he say?"

Sean cleared his throat. "I'm right here, ladies."

Maves stood and ruffled Sean's hair. "I know, kiddo." She winked at Aileen. "Have fun you two, I'll see you at practice."

As Maves headed out of the cafeteria, Sean slid into her empty seat. "Are you still eating?"

"No. I'm done."

"You only ate half your sub!"

"They're huge." She pushed the plate toward him. "Do you want the other half? I haven't touched it."

He reached for it. "Well, if you can't eat it..." He picked it up and took a bite. "I've never done as much training before. High school was nothing compared to this. I'm starving all the time."

"Did you run with a track club in high school?"

Sean shook his head. "Just cross country and track in the spring. It's crazy the mileage we were doing in the fall."

"Was it too much?"

"No! It's just different than high school." He took another bite and when he'd finished it he asked her, "What about you? Are you part of a club?"

"Mainly high school, but our track coach at my school started training me all year this year. I won state championships and qualified for Junior Nationals. Then did a couple more meets last summer."

"Cool. You'll love university track. It's *so* different. The school lets you pick your courses before the rest of the athletes so you can set classes around your training schedule. All the varsity athletes get to do that."

"Do you practice at different times during the week?"

"Always around three - three thirty. For Saturdays it depends on what part of the season we're in. The distance runners had some early long runs. I think the sprinters and jumpers usually train at nine. It's indoor season now so things are kind of all over the place. There's pretty much a meet every weekend. Sometimes two. The better athletes might go to one meet and then everyone else might compete in another."

"What year are you?"

"Freshman. But I grew up not far from here. My dad swam for UofG. I've been going to football games and campus fundraisers since I was a kid." He crumpled up his napkin and carried the tray to the rack by the door.

Aileen followed him. "Do you have a coat?" She slipped hers on and hung her backpack over her shoulder.

"Nah. I've got a couple layers on. He pulled a woolly hat out of his back pocket and a thin pair of gloves. "Is there anything you want to really see?"

"I don't know. Maybe the oldest building?"

Sean motioned to their right. "That would be the library. It was one of the first buildings established here. I think the French built it or something. It might have been here before the university itself was even built."

The main road in front of the Student Union turned into a walking pathway. They passed older buildings and some newer ones that had a modernist bent to them.

"The library's just behind the nutrition building," Sean said. "I'm majoring in dietetics. The square building in front of us is blocking the view of the entrance to the library. If you look above the square one, you'll see the bell tower and clock. It looks like a mini cathedral."

Aileen looked where he spoke and saw the large, now green, brass bell and a large clock on the other tower of the building. It looked like a miniature castle.

"Pretty cool, 'eh?"

She nodded.

"Inside there are still fireplaces that work. The track team has study hall Tuesdays and Thursdays and the room we're in has a big ol' fireplace."

"Study hall?"

"Freshman and transfers are required to meet twice a week to study or do homework. Once your GPA is over three point oh, you don't have to go. If your GPA drops, you're right back in."

"Is it just the track team?"

"All the sports team have scheduled study hall. Some on the same nights as us, some on different."

"Like the football team?" The post image of Tyler Jensen appeared in her head.

Sean chuckled. "Hell, no. Football has their own study hall."

By this time they had reached the library. Sean led her inside and showed her around. When they headed outside he asked, "What are you going take?"

"Probably Biology. Or something similar. I like science."

"I figured you for an Engineer."

"Really?"

"Nah." He motioned behind her. "We're just passing the Engineering hall and I'm starting to get cold. I was hoping we could go inside."

She laughed. "It is freezing, especially after walking by those nice fires."

He grabbed the sleeve of her coat. "Let's cut through then. We'll pretend I'm showing you the building. They're finicky and get mad when people come in that aren't there for class. It's distracting or something."

Aileen had the feeling he'd been asked to leave. After the shushing and dirty looks in the library from his constant chatter, she wouldn't be surprised if he'd been kicked out of a building or two. He was harmless and nice, and pretty funny. "What time do you have to be at practice?"

He checked his watch. "In about half an hour. We've got time to check out the biology building if you want. It's close by. Then we can stop by the outdoor track stadium before heading into Wavertree."

He stopped walking. "Do you want to see the football stadium? Or the dorms? I'm off campus but you would probably want to check out Holton House or Staple House. Staple House is where most of the athletes stay, but a bunch of the track athletes are at Holton House. It's closer to Wavertree."

She wasn't planning on going to Gatica so a look at the dorms didn't seem really necessary. The football stadium also didn't really interest her. It would be covered in snow and she highly doubted they would run into Tyler Jensen there. She would have better luck seeing him at track practice. Her heart raced at the thought of finally getting the chance to talk to him. "Do you mind if you head over to the Biology building? I'd really like to see it." It was only a little white lie. Right?

Chapter 4

"Success is a state of mind. Start thinking of yourself as a success."

Aileen read the words painted on the wall across from where she sat on the bleachers inside Wavertree Fieldhouse. The track team members were situated in groups all over the track. Hurdles were set up close by where she sat, the high jump apron was set, with some jumpers were doing run throughs, the distance runners were running in three groups on the inside two lanes of the track while sprinters were doing accelerations on the straightway across from her.

She liked how everyone laughed and joked around with each other. There were all these individual events, but in the chaos of practice, they looked like a team. Several athletes had stopped to say hello and introduce themselves. She felt bad that despite how friendly everyone had been, she couldn't remember all the names. She watched two girls head over to the starting blocks by the hurdles. Coach Anderson talked to them before pointing over to Aileen and waving.

She waved back and ran her fingers through her hair.

"I heard Sean took you around the school." Jani had one foot on a bleacher that was nearly as tall as her. She stretched her hamstring and grinned at Aileen. "Glad to see you survived. Did he hit on you?"

Surprised at the question, Aileen stuttered, "N-No. I-I don't think so."

Jani burst out laughing. "I was only teasing! I didn't mean to scare you." She switched legs to stretch her other hamstring. "After the meet tomorrow what do you feel like doing? Do you want to go see a movie... or do you feel like doing something a lot more fun?"

Aileen leaned back on the bench behind her and rested her elbows on it. Jani reminded her of Becky. "What do you have in mind?"

Jani glanced over Aileen's shoulder and then met her gaze. "Track party? Someone always plans one when we have a home meet. Tyler's throwing it tomorrow night."

"Tyler Jensen?" Aileen straightened and leaned closer to Jani, suddenly very interested in the party.

"The one and only. He's got this super cool old house off campus that he rents with some football players." She grinned slyly at Aileen. "Unless of course you prefer to just go to the movies or rent a DVD or something?"

"Hell, no." The words were out of her mouth before she could even process the thought. She was crushing on a boy she'd never met, drooling over his picture and now panting like an animal in heat over the possibility of going inside his house. What was going to happen next? Would she go and steal a pair of boxers?

Jani dropped her leg and grinned. "Good. I'm liking you more and more by the minute."

Another girl at the high jump pit called over, "Jani, you coming?"

Jani yelled back, "One sec." She turned to Aileen. "I've gotta measure out my approach. Tee can chat you up a minute." She gave Aileen an exaggerated wink and whispered, "Try to keep you knickers on."

Aileen watched her go, unsure what she'd meant by that last bit. It only took seconds for her to find out. The bleachers shifted as someone sat down a couple rows below Aileen. She glanced down and sucked in a breath.

Tyler Jensen. In the flesh. That beautiful mixed skin, covered in black and burgundy workout clothes, the back of his head showed his tight, curly hair cropped short against his perfectly shaped skull. Long, graceful fingers were busy tying his shoes.

He looked up as he finished and flashed her a smile. "Hey."

"Hey," she said in a breathy whisper.

"I'm Tyler."

"I know." She shook her head. "Sorry. I'm Aileen. Aileen Nessa. I'm visiting on a recruiting trip. I do the hurdles." She cringed inside. She sounded like an idiot. A babbling one.

He moved up to sit beside her and ran his eyes up and then down her again. "I know who you are."

"You do?" He smelled like an expensive musky cologne. It was probably deodorant but she would never forget that smell ever. She inhaled deeply and reprocessed what he had said. "You know me?"

"I watched you race at nationals this summer. You beat a friend of mine to get into the semi-finals."

"Oh, sorry about that."

He chuckled. "Don't be sorry. You looked a little lost in the race, hit the first three hurdles but managed to recover and still run a decent time."

She shook her head. "That was a crappy race. I was actually glad I didn't make the finals." Talking about track always helped her relax. She could talk about it forever.

"You made up for it a couple weeks later, I hear."

She shrugged. "It was my last meet of the season. I like trying to PR when it's the last one."

He gave her an appreciative nod. "Me, too!"

"You won NCAAs."

"I thought it was my last meet of the season." He touched his knee to hers. "I didn't think I'd be running last summer. So I had a crappy meet too."

"You came fourth... *at Nationals!*"

"Can I let you in on a little secret?" His beautiful eyes met hers and held her gaze. "I don't like to lose," he whispered, his warm breath brushing her cheek and ear like a feather.

He was so close she could see little specs of brown and almost yellow inside his blue-green eyes. She couldn't stop staring at them.

His eyebrows rose. "You okay?"

"P-Pardon?"

"Are you alright?"

Suddenly reality sunk in. She blinked and shifted away from him slightly. Her entire face burned, not just her cheeks. She knew her skin would be tomato red in color. Why did she always have to get so embarrassed? She'd just made a fool of herself. "I'm fine. Sorry." She bowed her head, letting her hair cover her face before finally looking out at the track. Anywhere but at him, praying the feeling of fire would leave.

"Tyler!" Coach Anderson called. "Let's go!"

He touched her leg. "I'll catchya later." Then he was gone.

Aileen felt the bleacher shift from his weight and watched him go from the corner of her eye. She was definitely not coming here next year. Either that, or she had better start working on being flirty and graceful. How come she could be so smooth and elegant on the track, but such a mess off of it? It was beyond annoying. She fought the urge to lay her head on her knees. No need to let anyone see that. As nice as they all were, they'd come rushing over to check on her. That was the absolute last thing she needed.

Coach Maves came into the field house. "Hi, Aileen. How did the campus tour go?"

Thankful for the distraction and friendly face, Aileen pushed her anxiety aside. "Sean did a good job."

"Great. I had a break so I went and checked you into your hotel room. I dropped your suitcase off in the room if that's alright." She pulled out a little envelope. "Here's your key cards for the room. You are in room one forty-eight. First floor."

"Thanks."

Maves pulled a small stack of papers stapled together and handed them to Aileen. "I've got to get working with the long and triple jumpers, but here's a copy of the girl's competing tomorrow. It shows all the schools and their best times this season. Thought you might like to look through it while we're practising."

"Sure." Anything to not focus on the conversation she had just had with Tyler Jensen. She also needed to stop referring to him as Tyler Jensen. They had been introduced now and he knew who she was. He was just Tyler. She needed him to be just Tyler.

When Maves headed to the other side of the track, Aileen watched her work with the athletes by her and also watched Coach Anderson at the starting blocks. Tyler worked out by him as well. He raced against the girls but his blocks where ten meters behind the girls. He also had four high hurdles set up while the girls had two, but really only went over the first one.

Tyler had pulled off his long pants and only wore a pair of shorts now. He had on an Under Armor long-sleeve, tight black shirt that seemed painted onto his flawlessly sculpted body. Aileen tried to focus on his form over the hurdles but she spent more time watching his abs and the rest of his muscles ripple in perfect synchronization. Even the two female hurdles spent more time staring than actually racing to the first hurdle.

Aileen flipped through the start time sheet Coach Maves had given her. There were only two UofG girls on the list and both of their times were okay. They were not superfast. Aileen hadn't competed in the 60m hurdles before, she had never done an indoor meet actually, so she didn't have her own times to compare to. However, the fastest girl on the list had competed last summer at junior nationals and Aileen had just beat her in the finals by one place.

She glanced over some of the other events and saw that Jani had the highest marked in the high jump. From the looks of it, she was a really good jumper, and it made sense, why else would a foreigner be on scholarship to an American university.

Practice lasted about an hour and a half. Maves drove Aileen to her hotel and told her Coach Anderson would be by around six thirty to pick her up for dinner.

Alone in the room and relaxing on the bed, Aileen skyped Becky.

"GIRLLLLL!" Becky screamed when she connected. "How is it? Are there as many cute guys as the brochure showed?"

"There's a few." Aileen laughed, happy to see her best friend.

"Did you talk to any?"

"Just one. The hurdler." She had no intention of rehashing the conversation. "He's having a party tomorrow night after the track meet. One of the girls on the team asked me to go."

"Are you?" Becky was straightening her hair as they chatted.

"Yeah, probably. I hope it's not like the one in Miami." Her recruiting trip to Miami had been a disaster. The two girls who took her out ended up getting so drunk, Aileen had to drive their car back. That whole trip had been a waste of time.

"It won't be. That's like lightning striking the same place twice."

"That can happen you know."

Becky laughed and shook her hair straightener at Aileen through the iPad screen. "If it's bad, find the cute guy's bedroom and crawl into his bed. When the party's over, he'll find you and then it'll be a recruiting trip you won't forget."

Aileen's first reaction was to shake her head, but the image that played out in her head didn't look so bad. Still, the embarrassing flush started to flood her skin and she had to shut the mental image down fast "It's not going to happen."

"Think of it as a backup plan. You should be doing a little recruiting yourself."

"Is that all you think about?"

Becky laughed. "I'm eighteen. Ninety percent of my brain can only focus on boys and music. The other ten percent likes sex and guitars." She made a face. "Not sex with guitars."

"That's disgusting." Aileen laughed despite herself. "You're the rocker and I—"

"—And you need to have someone rock your world. All you do is eat, sleep and breathe track."

"We'll see." She did not want to have this conversation now with Becky before having dinner with the head coach.

"Fine. I won't bug you. Just remember you picked this trip because of the cute guys. Let your hair down and have fun. You can embarrass yourself and don't have to care because you're not going there anyways. Promise me you'll do something a teeny-tiny bit crazy?"

Aileen laughed. "I promise."

"And you never break a promise."

"Never."

"Good. Now get a video of the hot guy running at the track meet tomorrow and send it to me. Then make sure you take some photos of him at the party." Becky burst into rocker mode, using her hair brush as a microphone and sang, "I want it all... I want it all."

"I didn't take my peeping-tom clothes but I'll see what I can do." She wanted a video of him racing herself, now she had the excuse to do it. "I gotta get ready. The coach is going to be here soon. I'll talk to you again tomorrow." She turned skype off as Becky continued rocking out to her hairbrush.

Chapter 5

Aileen showered and blew her hair out straight. She had packed a skirt and a dress to choose from, and decided to go with the skirt tonight. It was a black and white plaid kilt with red detail. Short, but still "politically correct", as Becky had told her when she helped her pack for the trip. She added a white button up top and thick tights so she wouldn't freeze her butt off.

If it snowed more she would be screwed tomorrow night with the dress. It wasn't exactly warm. She had a cool top and jeans she could wear as back up.

A knock reverberated against her door just as she finished putting her mascara on. *Perfect timing.* She gave herself a once over in the mirror and turned the bathroom light off. She grabbed her coat and tossed it on the bed to make it look like she had been waiting for Coach Anderson.

She checked the peephole to make sure it was the coach. She blinked in surprise when she saw two people out there.

Coach Anderson *and* Tyler Jensen.

Really?

Suddenly dinner was taking an interesting turn. She ran her palms against her skirt. Was she nervous? "Excited," she whispered as she tucked a lock of hair behind her ear. "I'm not nervous. It's no big deal." *Ha! Who am I trying to convince?*

She turned the handle and opened the door. "Hi, Coach Anderson. Just let me grab my coat." She spun around and tried to walk, not rush to the bed. The click of the door had her wincing when she realized she hadn't invited them in or given them a chance to hold the door for her. "Smooth move, dipstick," she mumbled to herself. She grabbed her coat and double checked that the hotel key was in her purse.

Straightening, she reopened the door and smiled. "Sorry about that."

Coach Anderson seemed oblivious to her mistake. "I invited another hurdler to dinner tonight. Thought it might be easier to ask another athlete what they think of the program." He patted Tyler's shoulder. "I think Tyler spoke to you earlier at practice."

Should she hold out her hand? Tyler stood beside the coach, his hands stuffed comfortably in his letterman jacket. He gave her a polite nod, and smiled. "Hope you don't mind a tag along."

Aileen knew she was staring again. She didn't mean to, but she couldn't stop herself. How could someone be that deliciously gorgeous? If Becky were here, she would flirt and know the perfect things to say. "I-It's fine. I d-don't mind at all." She lifted her coat to put it on.

Tyler stepped forward and held it for her to slip her arms through. Heat rose to her face but she pretended not to notice. "Thanks." She turned around and nearly got lost in those beautiful blue-green eyes again. They seemed more green-gray at the moment. Was that even possible? His eyes never left hers as if he was trying to figure out the same thing about hers.

Coach Anderson cleared his throat. "Shall we go?"

Aileen blinked and refocused.

They began walking down the hotel hallway toward the front entrance. Coach Anderson led the way while Tyler walked beside her.

"What kind of food do you like?" Coach Anderson asked as they stepped through the sliding doors of the front lobby to the cool night air.

"Anything is good with me." A gust of wind blew Aileen's hair back from her face. Did the wind ever stop? She shivered when Tyler moved closer to her.

"Winter's a bit fierce this year." He huddled inside his coat. "It's usually not this bad."

Coach Anderson drove a four door BMW. Aileen walked behind the coach and opened the backseat door. A drop of disappointment hit her when Tyler went around to the front passenger seat.

The car's heating system kicked on the moment Coach Anderson started it.

"There's a great restaurant in Campus Corner called Raw Hide. They serve steak, barbecue chicken, a bit of everything." Coach Anderson pulled out of the parking lot.

"Sounds good." She stared out the window at the passing night lights, sneaking peeks at the tall drink of water sitting in the front seat.

When Tyler turned to talk to her, she quickly adverted her eyes. "How many recruiting trips have you taken?"

"This is my last one."

His eyebrows arched. "Where have you all gone?"

"Stanford, Kansas State, LSU, and Miami."

Tayler chuckled. "You definitely picked the warm places. What made you come here?"

You. Though she was never going to admit that. Aileen tried to think of another reason that would be believable. "You've got a good biology program and," she grinned when a thought crossed her mind, "if Coach Anderson can turn you into an NCAA champion, I'd like to see what he can do with me."

Coach Anderson snorted. "She's got you there, Tyler. And she has faster times than you did coming into university."

Tyler crossed his arms, pretending to look mad. "Of course her times are faster, she's got ten meters less to run."

"No, I've compared her time and yours. Split them up so I could compare your hurdle to hurdle ratio. She's quicker than you were out of high school, comparatively speaking and taking into account other hurdles in your race at high school and college level."

Tyler put his arm across the seat and turned so he could lean closer to Aileen. "Coach Anderson's all about splits and times. He'll find some crazy angle or algebraic equation to figure sh— stuff out. You should see him calculate the way you need to set your blocks up!"

Coach Anderson smiled. "I don't hear you complaining when the times I predict match the times you run." He tapped his temple. "Besides years of experience, there's something up here that works."

Tyler dropped his arm from the seat. "It's that picture of me in your head." He shifted perfectly to dodge Coach Anderson's fist that swung out playfully to hit him.

Coach Anderson pulled into a parking lot dotted with cars. "You'll have to excuse Tyler. Since winning two awards last year, he seems to have lost all humility." He winked at Aileen through the rear view mirror. "That or hanging with the football players messes him up. It usually takes me three quarters of the indoor track season to get him off his high horse... just in time for the outdoor season."

Aileen listened to their banter and smiled. Just from today she could tell the athletes on the track team respected Coach Anderson because he was a good coach, but he also kept the playing field level for everyone. It sounded like no one got special treatment.

"Raw Hide is just around the corner." Anderson got out of the car and opened the door for Aileen. "I hope you are hungry."

"Getting there," she told him honestly.

They walked with Aileen in the middle of the two of them. As they reached the main street she recognized the road. The chauffeur had driven her down it earlier that day. She pointed to the old movie theater across the road. It looked pretty empty at the moment. "The guy who drove me down here said that was where the varsity sport kids hang out."

Coach Anderson chuckled. "It'll get busier later. Just without track kids tonight. If I see any of them down here after dinner, I'll have them doing a workout before the meet tomorrow."

"You won't see any footballers there." Tyler nodded to the building they were passing. "We hang at the First Down."

Aileen squinted as she tried to see through the dark windows. The place looked high end. She was beginning to think that footballers believed they were an entity unto themselves. She could imagine what Becky would say to that.

"Here we are." Coach Anderson pulled the door open to the Raw Hide.

The door handle was actually some kind of animal horn or antler. It matched the wood and rustic look of the interior design.

A large animal hide hung on the wall with pictures of bull riders all around it. Aileen inhaled a medley of savoury flavours, causing her stomach to rumble in agreement.

Tyler chuckled. "Glad to see you aren't a salad girl."

"I might be," she teased.

He shook his head. "No salad girl would close her eyes to enjoy the smell of steak cooking."

"Maybe I'm stopping to smell the potatoes." Really? Could she sound any cheesier?

Coach Anderson spoke to a waiter as he slipped out of his long coat. He still wore his suit. "Table is ready."

Tyler held out his hand to let Aileen go first. She followed the coach to a booth against the far wall. The restaurant's theme followed what she had seen in the front entrance. Wooden walls, more pictures of bull riders and barn items hung on the beams throughout the place. It actually looked pretty cool.

Coach Anderson slipped into one side, giving Aileen the spot with the best view of the restaurant and the window. Tyler sat down beside his coach. Aileen slipped out of her jacket and purposely shifted on the bench so she was sitting across from Tyler.

The waiter came with menus and filled their glasses with water. The coach and Tyler didn't open their menus. After a few minutes of looking over it, Aileen closed hers and folded her hands on the table. "I take it you guys come here quite often?"

Coach Anderson smiled. "They do a striploin that is delicious."

"I like the baseball steak," Tyler added. "Did you see something you like?"

Aileen ran her fingers through her hair. She didn't want to order the most expensive or the cheapest thing on the menu. The striploin was on the high end and the baseball steak seemed about in the middle. "I was thinking of trying the baseball."

Tyler clapped his hands. "Good choice!"

The waiter returned and took their orders.

Coach Anderson talked about Gatica's track program as they waited for their food. He told her about the conference they were in, how well they were doing, how their program was on the rise. Aileen tried to stay focussed on everything he was telling her. He compared the school to Stanford most of the time. When the food came, he said, "That's my lecture for the evening. How about we eat?"

Tyler pointed to the ball shaped steak on her plate. "Looks good?"

Aileen inhaled. "Smells good, too," she said and winked at him, surprised at her own cocky teasing.

"I deserve that." Tyler cut into his steak. "What does your family think about your recruiting trips so far?"

"My brother thinks I should go somewhere hot. My mom wants me somewhere close by and my dad, he's the only one who really gets it, he wants me to go where I can run. And get a good education at the same time." She added for the coach's benefit.

"I checked out Stanford and Miami on my trips."

"You did?" She was curious what he thought of the places.

"Loved Stanford." He twitched and Aileen had to stop herself from smiling when she realized Coach Anderson had kicked him under the table. "Didn't like Miami."

"Me, either!" She bit her tongue. This wasn't the place to gossip or admit that some of the girls on the Miami team had seemed mean and she didn't like the vibe she got from them. "It just isn't the place for me." She stared down at her plate embarrassed to have almost acted like a tattle tale.

"Well, we had better make sure Gatica is." Tyler rapped his knuckles gently against the table top.

Aileen brought her eyes up and held his gaze a moment before shifting to Coach Anderson. "How do you run your house here?"

"My house?"

"Wavertree Fieldhouse." She was kind of proud of her play on words. It made her feel like she had the upper hand in the conversation.

"Ahh..." Coach Anderson wiped his mouth with a napkin. "I like that. I might have to borrow it from you."

"It's all yours." Aileen did not miss the low chuckle that came from Tyler.

"Well then I guess I had better answer the question." Coach Anderson moved his plate and using his hands traced the shape of a track on the table. "The four hundred is basically four parts of a race. I approach the track season in a similar fashion. The first hundred," he said tracing the curve counter-clockwise, "is preseason training. School starts the last week of August and most of the track kids come the week prior. They start base training, which then gears more into technical training. It then switches to the next phase." He ran his finger over the straight away of the imaginary track. "Indoor season. For some, the season runs longer than others. That will be your case."

Tyler leaned forward and whispered, "He means NCAAs. He's pretty sure you'll make indoor nationals."

Coach Anderson ran his finger over the final curve of the track. "After indoor finishes, we move back into some base training and technical stuff. The curve is good to use as an example because it consists of different things. Competitive season is straight forward—"

"Like the straightaway," she finished.

"You got it." Coach Anderson moved his plate back to where it had been.

"Unless of course," Tyler said. "You're a cross country runner. Then you've got, like, six parts to a season. It gets complicated."

The coach smiled. "Yes, not every athlete followed the curve of the track. I just use it as a simple analogy." His phone began to ring. He reached inside his pocket and checked the caller. "Sorry kids, but I need to take this a moment."

Tyler slid out of the booth to let Anderson out. He sat back down after the coach had moved by the entrance where they had come in.

Aileen racked her brain for something intuitive to say. Here she had this moment alone with Tyler Jensen and she probably never would again. *Why do I always refer to him as Tyler Jensen? Why can't I just think of him as Tyler now?* She shifted on the bench and tried to appear relaxed. "What made you come here, Tyler?" *Jensen. Stop doing that!* "Why did you chose Gatica, say, instead of Stanford?" Good deep question. She was proud of herself.

Tyler sat back and put his arm over the back of the booth. If Aileen had the nerve, she'd have taken a picture with her iPhone. The guy could be a model.

"Stanford's a good school. Education, athletics, football... it's all there."

"And warm weather. Which is a bonus with training."

He nodded. "It is. However, I also like winter. The snow, tobogganing, all of it. New York gets all the seasons; all fall, winter, spring and summer. Stanford seemed to only offer a touch of spring and a lot of summer."

"You like winter?" Why would someone choose cold icy days like today when they could settle for weather... well, anything above freezing. "Where are you from?"

She swore she saw a twinkle in his eye when he grinned sheepishly. "Texas. San Antonio, Texas. It doesn't snow much there."

"So you basically chose Gatica for the snow?" She realized she hadn't heard an accent on him to give her a hint.

"When you put it that way, it sounds lame." He looked out the window and watched some fresh snow flakes fall. "I chose Gatica because I knew I would excel here. It felt like I belonged here. None of the other universities I looked at gave me that feeling."

She stared at him and a moment later made an effort to close her slightly hanging mouth. Beauty, brains and honesty. Yup, she could totally fall for him. She would definitely have to make NCAAs just so she could see him again next year. At Stanford, they wouldn't compete anywhere together until nationals. Maybe that was a good thing.

The waiter came by and asked if they wanted any desert. Aileen declined and then felt bad Tyler said no as well.

"You didn't have to say no on my account."

A single eyebrow rose on his face. "If I order something and you didn't, you're just going to stare with those puppy dog eyes of yours at my cheesecake and then I'd have to offer to share it with you. Then you'd get mad at me for ordering."

"I have a work out in the weight room tomorrow morning before the meet. Cheesecake won't hurt me any." *Puppy dog eyes?* She grew giddy from the silly compliment. "Do you always assume things about women?"

A sly look crossed his face. It made him incredible sexy. "Are you saying you aren't a typical woman?"

Wow, he had charisma. "I can't say I am... or I'm not. Comparing doesn't get you anywhere you really want to be."

"Except for hurdle times. You can compare there." He reached out and touched her wrist. "A pretty thang like you doesn't have to compare when you're already ahead of everyone else. Woman, or track-wise."

Coach Anderson approached the table and Tyler quickly sat back as if nothing had happened.

Which was probably true for him. Aileen, on the other hand, tried to suck in a few quick breaths without panting. She hadn't realized she had been holding her breath.

"I've already paid the bill," Coach Anderson said. "Is there anything else you'd like to see or do this evening, Aileen?"

Put the moves on your star athlete? "I think I'm good. I'll have an early start tomorrow morning if I want to get to the weight room before the meet starts."

"Yes, about that," Coach Anderson said. "I have to be at the track at least two hours before the meet starts. I can pick you up for seven-thirty or eight if you would like. I'll have one of the athletes come by and take you to the meet when you are finished."

"Okay. How about eight? Is that okay? I'll need about an hour and a half to get everything in. I can meet you down in the hotel lobby if that works?"

"Perfect."

Tyler helped her with her jacket when she fumbled trying to get it on. As they walked out into the cold, she fell instep beside him.

"Tyler!" A very large, muscular guy called out from the First Down as they passed it. The boy reminded Aileen of a fridge.

Tyler stopped walking. "Hold on a sec, coach." He jogged over to the entrance of the bar and chatted quietly with the guy who had called him. He came back a moment later. "Do you mind if I stay?" he asked Coach Anderson. He didn't even glance at Aileen. "Cody'll give me a ride home."

"No drinking. Don't be late. You've got a lot of eyes watching you." Coach Anderson glanced at Aileen.

"I know. I know." Tyler saluted Aileen. "Nice chatting with you tonight. I'm sure I'll see you tomorrow."

"Sure." She planned on secretly taping his race tomorrow so she could watch him anytime she wanted to. She watched him disappear into the First Down.

"Shall we get you back to the hotel?" Coach Anderson asked.

Chapter 6

Coach Anderson picked Aileen up exactly at eight as promised. She had only packed one set of workout clothes: a short pair of grey jogging shorts, long knee high socks, red t-shirt and a grey with red zip up sweater.

It looked super cute, kind of sexy, and if she was completely honest with herself, perfect to workout in.

She slipped a pair of loose jogging pants over her legs and pretended to be annoyed that more snow had decided to fall throughout the night. The freshly fallen soft white outside hung on the trees and made the ground bright and beautiful.

Coach Anderson drove his car into the parking lot in front of a building called Lord Warriors. Aileen saw the bleachers and press boxes from the football stadium behind the building.

She covered her head with her hoodie and tossed her backpack over her shoulder. "It looks like an awesome stadium."

"The press boxes were redone last summer. Student athletes get season tickets for all the home games. You haven't watched a football game until you've seen a homecoming game here in Gatica." He held the door open for her. "Do you have a weight room at your high school?"

She stepped inside and followed him down a hall. "Barely."

He smiled. "Then you're really going to like this one." He opened a glass door. "What do you think?"

The bright room reflected light and mirrors. In front of Aileen, was a row of slightly raised boxes. Bars with large weights lay on top of each step. The weights were red and black. Behind them, and against the mirrors, stood a line of free squat racks.

"It's pretty amazing."

A stocky man in a red polo shirt came jogging over. "Coach Anderson!"

"James, this is Aileen Nessa. She's going to be working out here this morning. Can you get her anything she needs?"

Aileen saw a look pass between the two of them that she couldn't decipher.

"No problem," James replied. He smiled at her. "Welcome to Lord Warriors."

"Sure." She pulled her hoodie off her head.

Coach Anderson opened the glass door again. "I'll see you back at Wavertree when you're done."

James pointed to the raised boxes. "What kind of stuff do you need to do, kiddo?" He wasn't much taller than her, but his voice boomed and echoed like a giant's. "Do you need the free weights?"

"It's mainly plyo box stuff. Do you have weight vests?"

James nodded. "You name it, we got it. Come on, I'll show you around." He began moving, not even bothering to check if she was following him. "This area is for all the Olympic lifting. Our footballers are on break since the season finished about a month ago. Right now they only lift three days a week and have the weekends off." A banging sound of metal on metal let them know someone was in the weight room already working out. "Around the corner here to the left is the bench area. Our footballers go hard here." He winked at her. "Glancing at your frame, I'm guessing you don't spend too much time on the arms."

She shook her head, not exactly sure what Olympic lifting was or why in world would she want to go 'hard' on her arms? A long, lean muscular body lay horizontal on one of the benches, his head obscured by the bench press in front of him. *Footballer.*

"Well if you decide to give it a try today, just ask Tyler over there to help you."

"Pardon?" Aileen was positive she had misunderstood him.

"If you want to try a bench press for fun," James repeated again, a bit slower and hard to believe, louder, "Tyler Jensen can help you out. Or I can."

At the sound of his name, Tyler sat up and looked over. He grinned and waved before wrapping a towel around the back of his neck. He marked something on a card and came over to them. "Hey, Aileen."

"Oh!" said James. "You two have already met?"

Tyler towered over James, wearing a perfectly fitted white tank top and black basketball shorts. "We have."

A phone began ringing in the office building on the far side of the room. "I'll be back in a moment." James jogged into his office and closed the door.

Aileen watched him go and tried racking her brain for something interesting to say. "How was First Down last night?" *Really? Why not just ask him if he hooked up? Better yet, does he have a girlfriend?*

"Fine," Tyler said, smiling at her. "What did you do?"

"Hung out at my hotel."

"Exciting."

She looked at him, purposely trying to avoid looking into his eyes. "Are you teasing me?"

He winked. "Maybe."

"Why are you here?" she blurted. "Shouldn't you be at the meet, warming up?"

He shook his head. "I'm out this indoor season. Football season ran a bit longer so Coach Anderson and I decided to give the indoor season a miss. It gives me an extra year if I decide to take it."

"Oh."

"So, coach's orders are that I train through and get ready for outdoors which stars in about three weeks." He shifted and glanced behind him. "James looks like he's going to be busy a while. What kind of workout do you have? Coach Anderson mentioned plyos?"

"Yes. Are there plyo boxes here?"

"Let me show you the way." He grabbed a bottle of water from a cooler and waited for her to follow. "Grab whatever you need from the fridge. It's football only, but I'll take the blame if you get caught."

"Thanks." She took a bottle of water even though she didn't need it and stuffed it in the side of her backpack.

They passed the Olympic lifting area and Tyler waved at James who gave him a thumbs up.

"Is he your football coach?"

Tyler chuckled. "James? Nah, he's way too nice. James is head of the weight training."

Aileen halted when they came into the back section of the weight room. A row of different sized plyo boxes lined two walls. More free squats with racks of large weights lined the other two.

"The far plyo box has vests, bosu balls, and balance stuff in it if you need any of that kind of stuff." He flashed her a grin. "Impressed?"

"Very." In all her recruiting trips she had never seen a room like this.

"Well, why don't you check out what you need and I'll get back to my workout. I told Coach last night I'd drive you over to him after." He patted her shoulder. "I'm in the other room if you need me. I'll tell James to let you work out. Just come get either of us if you need help with anything."

"Thanks." She appreciated that he offered to give her space. Ironically, she didn't care if others were in a room when she worked out, but the gesture to make her comfortable did not go unnoticed. When it came to sports, she became this entirely different person – confident.

She sat on one of the plyometric boxes and watched Tyler's retreating figure. He had a great ass and his long, sexy frame deserved to be appreciated. *Eye candy.* That's what Becky called good looking guys.

Sigh...and me with a sweet tooth. Her workout wasn't going to finish itself. She dug into her backpack and pulled out her earbuds, iPod with carrier to strap around her arm and her coach's list. Plyos and jump squats. He wanted her to use a weight vest. She walked by each of the boxes, amazed at the amount of boxes. Back home she had a two handmade ones by her coach, one foot and two foot. The boxes here were set up high, low, higher, low, and higher again, and then low and so on. The last box on the far end looked to be nearly as tall as her, maybe five foot. Who jumped that high onto a box?

Beside the last box in her row was a bin. There were weight vests, small weighted balls with handles and other larger ones the size of basketball. She rolled one of those over to see what it was. MEDICINE BALL 5KG. *Weighted balls. Cool.*

Not that she would be using those today. She picked up the five kilo vest, glad everything was labelled so it was easy for her to figure out what she needed. She set the vest by her backpack and hopped on a stationary bike to warm up.

Fifteen minutes later she was putting on the vest and slipping off her jogging pants. She switched her iPod to her workout music and checked her training. Twenty double leg jumps, ten single leg ones, drop to the floor for sit ups and push ups, repeat. She set her music to Superhero from the Script. She liked the song and it made her want to explode out of the blocks.

As she did her jumps she lost herself in the music and the rhythm her body created. She loved having the mirrors all around her. Not because she could stare at herself, but because she could watch her form, see if she was just going through the motions or pushing it as hard as she could. She never understood people who gave half effort. Everything had to be full out or nothing. Maybe that's what made her a good hurdler. When she was a kid, her mother always said it would get her places when she grew up.

Well, she was growing up and she wanted to make World Juniors in Bydgoszcz, Poland. She could go places with track and planned on making the most out of it. An education, travel, life experience, she didn't plan on missing out on anything if she had the ability to do it. No way.

She finished her last set of plyos and jumped up and down on the ground, bouncing to the music. She fist pumped and added a few dance steps in the excitement of being done. She froze when she saw Tyler in one of the mirrors. He stood leaning against the wall where it ended. His arms where crossed over his chest, his muscles perfectly curved and rounded in all the right places. His eyes were bright as he watched her.

"Hey," she said as she pulled an earbud out. She didn't have to worry about her face coloring, it was already warm and red from her workout.

His gaze slid from her eyes down her body and back up again. He smiled appreciatively. He tried covering his blatant checking her by asking, "How do you get your socks to stay up when you're jumping?"

She laughed. "It's these massive calves I have."

He glanced down. "They look pretty spectacular to me. They aren't massive, they're... perfect."

His compliment surprised her.

It must have surprised him as well. He quickly straightened and made his face unreadable. "I'm all finished. Didn't know how much more you had to do."

She reached for the string of her earphones and went to pull the other earbud out. It caught on something, probably her hair, so she tugged it harder. "I'm almo—Shoot!"

He stepped toward her. "What's wrong?"

She looked around her and checked her earbud. "I just pulled my earring out." She dropped to the ground to try to find it.

He crawled over to her. "What's it look like?"

"Gold hoop with a diamond on it."

"Wow, that's some nice boyfriend." He kept his head down, his hand running over the grey Berber carpet.

"They're from my grandmother. An early graduation present." She smiled at his comment. "I don't have a boyfriend."

"I'm surprised. I would think the guys at your school are lining up to date you." He bent slightly to check under a plyo box.

She giggled. "No one's lining up. I'm from a small town. Everyone knows everybody since third grade." She swallowed, suddenly very aware of how she was sounding. "It's not that I haven't dated. Or had a boyfriend. I have. I just... I just wanted to focus on school and hurdles this year." She didn't feel the need to mention the last boy she dated had cheated on her. She had walked in on him making out with another girl from school at a party. Kind of embarrassing. She held her breath, not sure if she should ask him the same question. She bit her lower lip then blurted, "What about you? Do you have a girlfriend?" She was positive there were a million girls chasing after him.

He sat up on his knees. "I had a girlfriend last year. It's just hard. Between football and track. Things went really well last year and there were some big expectations I needed to focus on. Then I won NCAAs last year, I wasn't expecting that."

Aileen pictured some cheesy cheerleader with pompoms on her hips all mad because Tyler wasn't giving her much attention. "You won some football thing last year too, right?"

Tyler chuckled. "The Jim Thorpe Award? It was this year actually."

"Oops. Sorry. Congrats."

He smiled. "Thanks." He squinted just passed her. "Is that your earring?" He pointed by the other row of plyo boxes.

Aileen crawled over, not realizing that Tyler did the same thing. Their heads bonked into each other.

"Shit! Are you alright?" Tyler reached for her forehead and rubbed it lightly.

It hurt. It felt like the guy had a metal plate in his head and they'd barely hit each other. His fingers felt like magic against her skin. They were cool, slightly rough but gentle. "I'm okay." She stayed on all fours not wanting to move away from his touch.

A sparkle of light from the ground caught her attention. "My earring!" She had to lean toward Tyler to pick it up. His face was inches from hers. She could feel his warm breath brush against her face. Her fingers hesitated over her earrings as she met his gaze. She swallowed hard and her eyes flitted down to his soft lips before dropping down to the floor. If she leaned just a little bit closer... she could just brush her lips against his for just a moment...

Taking a deep, slow breath, she forced the moment to pass. Her fingers curled around her earring. She was crazy to even think he might be interested in her, a silly recruit. "Found it!" She sat back and held up her earring.

Tyler blinked and blinked again. "Does it have a backing?"

She shook her head as she clipped the earring back in place. "It's pierced with one of those bars that click into the other part. See?" She turned her head to show him the earrings.

Silent, he reached out and touched her, letting his finger trail down her neck before dropping his hand suddenly and stood up. "If you're, uh, finished, we should get going to Wavertree then." He walked toward the junction of the room where the Olympic weights were. When he turned around his face was unreadable.

A whirlwind of emotions ran through Aileen. She couldn't believe how bad she wanted to kiss him. Thank goodness she hadn't!

She stood and grabbed her stuff. Suddenly the weight room seemed too hot, stuffy and small. She needed to get outside for some fresh air.

She nearly stumbled as she realized she would be climbing into his car and sitting right beside him as they headed over to

Wavertree. Her stomach felt like it was going to burst from the sudden storm of butterflies beating around inside of it.

Chapter 7

Neither of them spoke as they stepped outside. The parking lot had a number of cars in it, though Aileen had only seen Tyler and James inside. Obviously there was more to the building than she had seen. She tried guessing which car might be Tyler's.

Tyler cut across the lot, heading towards a red sports car that stood out bright against the snow. She moved to go around to the passenger side and was surprised when he kept walking. She followed on the other side of the car, too embarrassed to say anything.

Behind the red car was a black car which blended in with the recently plowed parking lot.

The hood had a raised center. The car was old. Not the vintage collector's old, but the seventies or eighties kind of old. She knew nothing about cars.

Tyler jogged around and unlocked her door. "Pretty cool, 'eh?"

She slipped into the passenger seat as he came around the car to his. "It's, uh, interesting."

He turned the engine a few times before it finally kicked in and roared to life. "Interesting?" He ran his hand over the dashboard. "She's a beauty."

Noticing the Ford emblem on the steering wheel she shrugged. "I'm sorry. What is it?"

"It?" Tyler tutted and shook his head. "It's a she. She's a nineteen-eighty Ford Mustang Cobra."

"It's a Mustang?" She hadn't noticed the horse on the front of the hood, just the raised center part.

He nodded.

At least the seats were cloth instead of pleather. Otherwise, she would be freezing her butt off even more than the shivering she was doing at that moment. With all the goose bumps the cold air was giving her, she'd have to shave again soon.

Tyler put the car into drive and spun the tires as he pulled out of the parking lot.

Aileen grabbed the dashboard, positive the car was going to slide into a ditch or tip over.

"It's got winter tires, and just because it's from the eighties doesn't mean it's going to fall apart." He laughed. "I bought it with next to no miles on it. I've had it since I started my first year of university. I'd saved up for school and when I got a scholarship, I treated myself." He slowed down and turned the heater on high. "I bought it in Texas and drove it up here. It was a friend of my mom's. She had gone through this nasty divorce way back. Her husband had cheated on her and all that crap. She ended up with the house and his car. She kept it in the garage for almost twenty years. When she heard I was car shopping, she told my mom she had something I might like. So I got a steal of a deal, worked on it all summer, then drove it up here."

"Is it a chick magnet, like you hoped?" She giggled and leaned away from him as she teased him.

"Pardon?" He kept his eyes on the road, but glanced at her through his peripheral vision.

"Wasn't that your hope? That the car would attract chicks like a magnet?" She had no idea what she thought it was so funny. Maybe the pent up frustration from inside the weight room had messed with her head. "It seems more like a grandpa car to me."

"What?" You're kiddin', right?" He tenderly touched the dashboard again. "Don't listen to her, baby. She doesn't know what she's talking about!"

Aileen burst out laughing again. "You talk to her?" She brought her hand across the dashboard from the window toward the radio. "I hope he treats you well, grandma." Her hand accidently brushed against his. A shock sparked when they connected and ran up her arm. She jerked her hand away in surprise and then tried to cover it up by slipping both her hands under her legs and sitting on them. She pretended to shiver, but it had nothing to do with the cold.

Tyler turned the heater up higher. "She's not a grandma," he insisted.

Aileen tried not to smile, but the more she tried the more she couldn't stop laughter from escaping. "Sorry. Do... you... call her N-Nanny, then?"

They came to a red light. Tyler stopped the car and shifted so he was completely facing her.

She noticed he was trying to keep a straight face but the corners of his mouth kept turning up.

"This baby is not a grandma, or a nanny or gran or anything related to that. She's a sleek, revved up, hot—" He paused when the car suddenly stalled.

Aileen fell back against her seat, a fit a giggles were now making her ab muscles sore. "You were saying?"

He turned the key in the ignition and luckily it kicked back to life instantly. "Can't even back me, baby?" he mumbled to the car.

It only made her laugh harder. Tears were rolling down her cheeks. She wiped at her eyes paranoid black smudges from her mascara would give her a raccoon look. "Maybe she wants a name? Gertrude?"

Tyler's eyebrow cocked up. "What kind of name is Gertrude?"

"Not the right one for your baby? How about Elizabeth?"

He pointed a finger at her. "Too long."

"Beth? Liz? Lizzy?" She tried shortening. "I can't believe you've had this car for three years and never named her." It took everything not to laugh. Hopefully he would think she was coming around to his way of thinking.

"I like Lizzy." He patted the dashboard. "What you think, baby? Shall we christen you Lizzy?"

Aileen nodded. "It totally suits her." She had no intention of telling Tyler that her grandmother's name was Lizzy.

"Just for the record," he said as he pulled into an open parking spot by Wavertree. "She never stalls." He cut the engine and leaned close to Aileen before whispering, "I don't think she likes you very much."

Aileen leaned toward him, unclicking her seatbelt and pressing one hand on the car's door handle. She brought her head close to his. She whispered back, "You can tell her the feeling's mutual." Then she jumped out the car before Tyler could grab her.

He was out of his seat and around the car before she had a chance to realize. "Did you forget something?" He held her backpack up high, just out of her reach.

She jumped up and swiped at it just as he twisted his upper body so she wouldn't get it. Her hand landed against his chest instead. She could feel the firm muscles clearly under his coat. "You're such a tease." She tried reaching to get it again – unsuccessfully.

"I am? What were you doing inside the car?"

Her hands went to her hips. "Trying to be polite to my chauffeur so he wouldn't make me walk in the cold back here."

He pointed a finger at her. "You are so bad!" He grinned and handed the backpack over to her. "For a blond girl, you've got a lot of common sense."

She punched him in the gut, his rock hard abs flexing instantly to protect him. "Hey! Watch it!"

Both of Tyler's hands went up in mock surrender. "I was just kidding."

She cocked her head to one side. "So who's the tease now?"

"Okay, okay. Can we call it even?" He held his hand out to her. "Truce?"

"For now." She slipped her hand in his, enjoying the tremor of something sensational cruise up her arm and settle deep inside her. She wondered momentarily if he had the same feeling. His hand felt wonderfully warm against hers. She shivered, not realizing she wasn't dressed for the weather and had grown cold.

Her hand still in his, Tyler pulled her to him. "Let's get you inside before you freeze to death." He stayed close to her and dropped her hand. "That'll make it near to impossible to get you to sign with us if that happens. Coach won't be too impressed with me if I let you die of cold right outside the field house."

Aileen lost the ability to speak. A wave of mysteriously exotic cologne filled her nostrils when Tyler pressed her close. She didn't want to move away and lose the stimulating scent. No guy should ever smell this good.

They walked to the same side entrance she had arrived at yesterday.

"Is Jani taking you out tonight?" Tyler asked once they were inside and heading down the hallway to the indoor track. As they got closer, the sound of track life grew louder and louder. Cheering, the start gun, all of it sounded like music to Aileen.

"Yeah." She wondered if and how she should mention she knew about his party. "What year is Jani?"

"She's a sophomore. Did you know she's one of the best jumpers in Canada?"

"Wow. Impressive. She seems really nice."

"She is." He pulled his phone out of his coat pocket and checked the screen. "Did she tell you there is a track party tonight?"

"At your place?"

He grinned. "She told you." His phone vibrated against his hand. "I'm leaving early with a couple of the guys to set everything up. Once we're inside here, I don't know what Coach Maves or Anderson has all planned for you so if I don't see you before I go..." He hesitated. His eyebrows pressed together as he looked at her uncertainly. "You are coming to it, right?"

"Whatever Jani wants to do, I'll tag along." He wanted her to come. Why she had the sudden urge to stamp her feet really fast and scream with excitement, she had no idea. It was a totally new feeling to her.

"Jani's coming. She wouldn't miss it."

Neither would I. "Then it looks like I'll be there—."

"Tyler!!" A large voice boomed. "Get in here!" A solid, had to be shot-putter or hammer thrower stood at the entrance to the indoor track. "Bring your tiny, cute friend along too."

Tyler rolled his eyes. "Jason, this is Aileen. She's here on a recruiting trip."

"Sweet." Jason clapped his hands and chalking white powder floated into the air. "You coming tonight?" He gave her a bone crushing hug.

Definitely a shot putter. Aileen couldn't talk, let alone breathe. He finally put her down after he'd carried her inside the field house. The indoor track was full of life. She forgot about answering Jason as she got lost in the moment. The sixty-meter sprints were in progress. Running through what she remembered of the schedule, she realized that the hurdle races would be next.

"Let's get a good seat to watch the finish," Tyler touched her elbow and steered her in front of several rows of bleachers. "By the way, I'll make sure Jani keeps you away from Jason. The big guy is awesome, but he has this thing about lifting people."

Aileen laughed. "I thought he was going to smother me."

Their progress to Tyler's chosen spot slowed. People on the bleachers called out Tyler's name and Aileen swore every other person wanted to talk to him.

At the third set of stands, Coach Maves appeared. "Perfect timing. Let me take you infield so you can watch the races close up."

"Okay" The worst thing in the world for Aileen was being at a track meet watching her event and being unable to compete. She itched to be at that starting line, getting ready in the blocks when the hurdle race started. She turned to say good-bye to Tyler but three girls from another school were now standing between them. It was more than a roadblock. It was a wake-up call. She was wasting her time. If she thought he was cute, so did probably ninety-nine per cent of the population. What was she thinking? She didn't stand a chance. No chance at all.

Chapter 8

The meet continued on through the day. Coach Anderson spoke to her towards the end of the meet and told her he would pick her up for breakfast the next morning at nine. Her flight was scheduled for the late afternoon. He wanted to talk about what the school and track program had to offer her before she left.

Jani won the high jump. The loud speakers told Aileen that Jani had qualified for nationals with a six foot jump. She had no experience with high jump, but it seemed pretty high to her.

On a high from the competition, Jani came bouncing over to where Aileen sat. "You ready to get out of here?"

Aileen nodded and grabbed her backpack.

"My car's parked by the student union. The party starts in like two hours. Do you want to go shower, get ready and then go eat? Or do you want to eat, then go get ready?"

Her stomach rumbled.

Jani laughed. "I guess that means you want to eat first?"

"I had lunch forever ago. I'm more of a grazer, I like to eat constantly."

Jani put her arm around Aileen's shoulders. "You're a girl after my own heart. Pizza sound good? There's an awesome place in Campus Corner that makes awesome brick oven pizza. It's so good." Jani's midsection growled.

Aileen burst out laughing. "My grandmother used to say that a tummy never lies."

"It doesn't. You're gran's a smart cookie." She pulled out her keys and a pair of lights flashed by them. "You worked out this morning in the weight room, I heard. Who dropped you off here?"

Aileen tried to appear nonchalant as she got in Jani's car. She shrugged. "Tyler. He was working out and then drove me over."

"Tyler? Interesting..."

"Why?"

"Tyler's football. Yeah he runs track, but he's football through and through."

"What do you mean?" He hadn't seemed all football to her.

"He doesn't partake in the recruiting trips."

"He doesn't?" Aileen tilted her head. "He came out for dinner last night with Coach Anderson and me."

Jani slammed on the breaks. "What? Coach Anderson *really* wants you here. He's pulling out the big guns." She began moving forward again. "Did Tyler have his car or coaches?"

"His. It's a Mustang snake or something."

Jani giggled. "You mean Mustang cobra?"

"Yeah." She waved her hand. "If Tyler's all football, then why is he throwing a track party?"

"He loves track and doesn't act like he's above anyone. That's one of the reasons why everyone loves him." Jani elbowed her when she rolled her eyes. "It has nothing to do with his beautiful body and handsome face. But Tyler's successful, he's good for the school, good for the sport, he's the face of UofG at the moment. Coach Anderson doesn't ask Tyler to do recruiting stuff." Aileen frowned, trying to make it all make sense in her head. Jani, patted her hand. "It's not a big deal." She found a parking spot outside of a restaurant with large glass windows showing brick ovens on the far wall. "Let's go eat before we starve!"

Inside they ordered and settled onto bar stools that lined the entire place. They chatted track while they ate. Aileen really liked Jani and pulled her phone out to add her email and social networks. She hoped to stay in touch after she left.

Back in the car, Jani headed toward Aileen's hotel. "What do you want to do now? Get ready at the hotel and I pick you up on the way to the party? Or do you want to grab your stuff and get ready at my place? We can hang out and have a laugh. My roommate, Linda, is a long jump / triple jumper. She's coming too. It's my turn to drive. I won't be drinking. Well, maybe one drink or two, tops."

Aileen had been hanging with Becky at bars where the band played for the past two years. She wasn't much of a drinker, but she had been around it enough that it didn't bother her. The party sounded like it was pretty much going to be the same thing; stuck in a room full of people who she didn't really know. Hopefully the music would be as good as Becky's band.

She realized Jani was waiting for an answer. She felt more comfortable getting ready at the hotel on her own, but she didn't want to disappoint Jani. "Do you want to grab Linda and get ready at my hotel?"

Jani flipped on her blinker and made a sharp turn. "Awesome idea!"

Aileen held onto the door handle, paranoid the little car was going to flip over. What was with the driving here in Gatica?

Jani zigzagged through streets and pulled into a drive with a yellow house. She pointed up the road, the opposite way they had come. "School's right over there. I lived at the dorms my first year and that was enough. This little place is great. Two girls on the volleyball team, myself and Linda are here." She threw the front door opened and hollered out, "Linda, grab your stuff!" She tossed her keys on the table just inside the door. "One of the girl's graduates this year so we are going to have to find a new roommate. There are 4 rooms. Two upstairs, two down." She pounded on the door connected to their living room. "Linda!"

A girl about the same height as Aileen walked out of the kitchen, toothbrush in her mouth. "Whath'up?" She barely gave Aileen a glance.

Aileen remembered seeing her at the track meet earlier. She closed the outside door and leaned against it.

Jani headed across the living room. "Aileen's offered to let us get ready at the hotel. It'll be fun. Grab your stuff and let's go." She disappeared in the kitchen. "Aileen, my room's at the back. Just let me grab my stuff. Have a seat. TV remote's around there somewhere."

Aileen sat on the arm of the coach, unsure what to do. She watched Linda roll her eyes and shake her head. She went chasing after Jani. Aileen tried not to listen but with the thin walls, it was hard not to.

"I'm not going! That girl's in high school! She's like what? Sixteen?"

"Eighteen, almost nineteen. She's cool."

"I made us *drinks!* We can't feed her vodka and Kool-Aid! She's going to be a stick in the mud. Seriously, why did you tell coach you would take her tonight, of all nights?!"

"I wanted to and coach asked me. She's a really, really good hurdler. Tyler Jensen wants her at the school as well. He did dinner with coach and her last night. Then Aileen said he was working out in the weight room this morning and took her back to Wavertree."

"So?"

"Linda, you're impossible! Stay here and get ready then. I'm going with Aileen. It'll be fun to get ready at a hotel."

"How am I going to get the party then?"

Jani laughed. "That's your problem. I'm leaving and you are welcome to come with us. Take your drink as a traveller."

An exasperated sigh muffled through the walls. Aileen assumed it came from Linda. She wished she had just had Jani drop her off instead of going through this. She didn't like annoying anyone.

The two girls appeared, Jani with a backpack and Linda with a sour look on her face. She stomped by Aileen and slammed the door to her room.

Aileen glanced, wide eyed at Jani. "You can bring me back if it's easier."

"No!" Jani shook her head and dropped into the seat close by Aileen. "Linda's just being a bitch."

"I heard that!" Linda yelled from her room.

"Well stop acting like one so I don't have to tell people!" Jani shouted back.

Aileen cringed. These girls were crazy.

Jani leaned her head against Aileen's side. "She'll be totally fine when we get to your hotel. Just wait. She's all nails and hissy-fits and then calm as a kitten."

True to Jani's words, when they finally got back to the hotel and started getting ready, Linda relaxed. She warmed up to Aileen and began joking and laughing as they did their hair.

Aileen wasn't sure if it was because of the Kool-Aid vodka Linda was drinking, or something else. She seemed completely different than Jani, who was genuinely friendly and nice. Linda had an edge about her that struck Aileen as hard. She had a feeling that if you crossed Linda, she would never let it go. Maybe it made her a better competitor.

Aileen showered and changed in the bathroom. She blow dried her hair quickly, wearing it wavy instead of straight. It would take too long to straighten and she didn't want to hog the bathroom. She slipped into her black dress and assessed her figure in the mirror. The dress had three quarter sleeves and an open neck. It ended just by her knees and hugged her body in all the right places. She liked the black against her blond hair. She had a pair of fitted high black boots that went perfect with them.

All she needed was her silver necklace that Becky had bought her at Christmas. It was half a heart that fit perfectly into one Beck wore around her neck.

She stepped out of the bathroom to grab it.

Jani whistled at her. "Whoa, girl. You. Are. Smokin'!"

She glanced down, it wasn't sexy or even remotely slutty. Linda on the other hand had a black skirt on that barely cover her assets. Her matching turquoise blue tank top was covered in glitter.

Jani had a red dress on that clung tightly to her. She was so tall, the dress probably would have reached anyone else's knees. On her, it came mid-way down her thighs. She spread her hands over her chest. "I have no boobs. I'm so jealous you have perfect perky ones, Aileen. You know people pay big money to get theirs to look like that."

Linda sputtered grape liquid down her chin as she tried not to laugh. She ran to the bathroom, her hand covering her mouth.

"Th-thanks, I think." Aileen didn't know what to say.

"You look really... classy." Jani smiled and tried to pull her dress down a bit. "You're very pretty. I can see why Tyler's interested."

Tyler interested? In her? Aileen blinked, trying to process Jani's words.

"Stop hitting on the recruit!" Linda moaned as she came out of the bathroom. "Don't scare the poor thing." She came wobbling out of the bathroom in a pair of six-inch heels. How Aileen had missed them before, she had no clue. Linda lifted Aileen's hair and patted it back down into place. "Jani likes boys. You don't have to worry."

"Okay." Aileen stepped just out of reach of Linda's wandering hand. She was drunk already. The girl wasn't going to last until midnight at this rate.

"Let's get this party started!" Linda grabbed her large traveller mug with its twirly straw and waited by the door.

Chapter 9

They had to park the car a block from Tyler's house. The party was in full swing, spilling out to the lawn and laughter carried over to where the girls had parked.

Linda tossed her coat into the car. "I'm not going to try and find it later." She crossed her bare arms over her nearly naked belly. She seemed oblivious to the cold. She marched in front of Jani and Aileen.

"Tyler's place has, like, eight bedrooms. Last year he threw the party this same weekend and had a room set for coats. Even had a rookie football player manage a coat check."

"Really?" Aileen snuggled into her jacket, wondering how many people where actually going to be there. "Does Tyler live with any other track members?"

Jani shook her head. "A couple of footballers. Eight bedrooms and only four guys live there. They each get two rooms. So lucky. I'd make one into a closet."

"That would be cool. Put a door between the two rooms and tell everyone you have a walk in."

Jani clapped her hands. "Exactly!"

They came to the house. There was a park to the right of the house and a large garage on the other side and then the neighbour's house that was dark. Tyler's house was massive. It was an old heritage home, probably around when the north fought the south.

"Do footballers get more money that other scholarships?" She wondered how he afforded living in a place like this.

"Nope. It's all the same. I heard the guy who owns the house used to play football for Gatica. He's a big alumni supporter and played in the NFL. He probably rents it to the football players for next to nothing."

"Lucky."

Music blaring from a stereo on the front porch stopped any chance of hearing a conversation. The music bounced off her chest and blasted into her ears. Aileen covered her ears as they made their way across the wrap around porch to the side entrance. It lead them into a crowded, high ceiling kitchen.

"I thought you said it was a track party?" Aileen asked Jani as she watched Linda push her way through people towards a keg.

"It is, plus a few friends." Jani winked. "If it's too busy, just say the word and we'll head out."

"Thanks." She tried not to appear obvious as she searched the kitchen for Tyler. It was his party, she should say hello when she saw him.

Jani grabbed her arm, and a bowl of chips off the counter. "Come on, let's introduce you around."

The hallway that lead out of the kitchen opened to a winding staircase that had a balcony above which over looked the large front entrance below. This house was unbelievable.

"Aileen!! Aileennneee!" someone called down from the second floor.

She looked up and saw Sean weaving his way by people and then down the staircase.

"I can't believe you came!" He hugged her.

"I can't believe you aren't wearing your red coat costume!" She gestured at his jeans and button up shirt.

Jani burst out laughing. "You've been here two days and you've already seen the red coat get up? Which one? Sean's got like five of 'em."

"I only have three!" He looked down. "Do you lovely ladies need a drink?"

"We're not drinking tonight."

THE RECRUITING TRIP

"Not even coke? There's a machine in the kitchen that's got some fruit punch concoction that is non-alcoholic." He pointed his thumb behind his shoulder. "I'll go grab you one."

He wasn't going to give up. "Yes, please." At least holding a cup would have something to do with her hands.

"Me, too," Jani added. "Thanks."

"My pleasure." He bowed dramatically. "If you make your way to the living room, there's a dance floor already bustin' a groove." He saluted and then disappeared into kitchen.

Aileen thought she saw Tyler upstairs behind some people leaning against the railing. She strained her neck trying to get a better look.

"Do you like dancing?" Jani asked her.

She did, she just wasn't sure she wanted to head onto the dance floor at this party. Her heart missed a beat when she saw Tyler coming down the stairs. It was him before, at the top of the stairs. He had on a grey polo shirt that made his eyes look brighter than usual. Even his dark jeans seemed like they were made just for him.

He smiled and waved when he saw her. A girl on the stairs stopped him and began talking. He listened and responded to her, but his eyes kept shifting over to Aileen.

"What are you guys still doing here?" Sean came back carrying three drinks. He handed each of them a cup, keeping the one full of beer for him. "I thought Jani would be tearing up the dance floor by now."

Jani elbowed Aileen. "I'm just waiting for Aileen to decide if she wants to stay here watching Tyler or come along."

Aileen's face burned instantly. "I wasn't..." She had no idea how to finish that sentence and when Tyler began coming down the stairs, she grabbed Jani's hand and pulled her toward the living room trying to move fast and beat Tyler before he made it down the stairs. She was way too embarrassed to talk to him now. "Let's go dance!"

"I thought you'd never ask!" Jani teased.

They slipped in between people as they made their way to the dance floor. The living had the same high ceiling and the furniture had been pushed against all the walls. A DJ had a corner with the only light in the room besides the strobe lights flashing on the middle of the floor. It was crowded but because of the size of the room, there was plenty room to dance.

Jani stepped in front of Aileen and found a spot big enough for them to move around and dance. She was glad Sean had managed to stay with them and began moving the minute a new song came on.

From where she stood, Aileen had a clear view of the entrance to the living room. When Tyler came into the room she dropped her gaze and focussed on what Jani and Sean were doing. She had taken jazz, pop and every other dance class as a kid, and it came to her rescue now.

She tried to get lost in music but she could feel Tyler's eyes on her as he made his way toward them. He was a popular guy. People constantly stopped him to talk or high five him or offering him a drink. She tried not to watch, but couldn't stop herself.

After the fifth song they had danced to ended, Aileen was hot. She pulled her three quarter sleeves up and wished she could take her boots off. Her drink was long gone. She tapped Jani on the shoulder. "I'm going to grab a drink. Do you need another one?"

Jani nodded. "Yes, please." She glanced around, her eyes pausing a moment on Tyler who was watching them. "Do you want me to come?"

"I'm okay. I'll be right back."

Jani turned back to Sean and grabbed his hands. "Show me your moves, skinny man."

Aileen slipped behind a group dancing beside them and attempted a detour as she tried to avoid bumping into Tyler. If Jani hadn't said anything, she would have been fine. Except,

THE RECRUITING TRIP

Aileen kept thinking about what Jani had said at the hotel, and then her comment here. *I'm on a recruiting trip. Not trying to hook up with a guy. That's totally not me.* Why was she trying so hard to convince herself? Did it really matter?

She paused in the hallway as a cool breeze teased her hot skin. The front door was open but nobody was using it. She stepped out onto the porch and headed right. People stood laughing and talking on her left, which would bring her around to the kitchen. She just wanted a moment alone to catch her breath and maybe gather her thoughts.

She walked around the corner to an empty spot of the porch. Only a bench stood against the side of the house. She ran her hand along the limestone and could feel the base of the music from the living room beating against it. The music came out muffled and quiet, the stone absorbing most of the sound.

"Are you avoiding me?" Tyler's voice came out teasing behind her.

She spun around, surprised.

He stood a few feet away, hands in his dark jean pockets, his chest muscles pressing against his shirt, grinning at her. The guy could be a model. He probably was.

"You're a popular guy."

"I am?"

"Every time you take a step, someone has to come up and talk to you."

His grin turned into a sexy smile. He took a step closer to her. "Have you been watching me?"

She wished she had pockets so she had something to do with her hands. She played with the pendant on her necklace instead. "Maybe. Have you been following me?" Where did this boldness inside of her come from when he was around?

"Maybe." He took another step, now they stood less than a foot apart. His gaze wondered from her eyes to her mouth.

She ran her tongue over her lips and held her breath. For a moment it seemed like they were the only two people in the world.

"I really want to kiss you." His bold statement made her gasp slightly. "I just don't know if I should." He ran a hand over his short hair, pausing at his neck. "I feel out of control when I'm around you. Like I want to let go of everything and just... just... kiss you." He moved so there was no space between them.

Aileen dropped her arms to her sides and closed her eyes as she brought her head up toward his. She felt his warm hands fit perfectly into hers. His lips brushed against hers softly and she heard herself sigh. He pressed his mouth against hers with more urgency, his hands sliding up her forearms, his fingers curling around her elbows.

He slowly let his mouth move away from hers as he rested his forehead against hers. "I shouldn't have done that. I'm sorry."

"Don't be sorry. I'm not," she whispered.

"This isn't right. I'm not the calm in a storm you'd be looking for, I'm the shipwreck that'll take you down." He sighed. "And now I'm quoting songs."

"Aileen?" Jani's voice called out from the front of the house.

Tyler jumped back as if he had been bitten. He ran his thumb over his lower lip, as if trying to rub any possible lipstick away. He cleared his throat.

"She's right here, Jani." He called over his shoulder, his face and body language completely unreadable now.

Aileen hoped she didn't look as frazzled as she felt on the inside. She flipped her hair over her shoulder, thankful the night shadows would hide her face.

Jani slowly came around the corner, her arm around Linda holding her up. "I think we, uh, gotta go."

"I don' feeltho 'hood," Linda mumbled, her words barely coherent.

"Crap!" Tyler grabbed Linda around the waist as she feel forward. "How about we take a little walk around the porch here. Get some fresh air inside of you?" He basically carried Linda as they walked down toward the back of the house and turned around again. "What she been drinking?" he asked Jani.

"Purple Kool-Aid and vodka."

He grimaced. "Have you been drinking it too? Either of you?"

Aileen and Jani both shook their heads.

"I think she's going to need to lie down—" Tyler said.

"I'm bine," Linda cut him off and lurched away from his suddenly, running to the edge of the porch. She leaned over and vomited.

The stench of it wafted over to them. Jani dashed over to help Linda by holding her hair back. "Go away, bitch!" she barked at Jani. She lifted her high heeled foot and shoved Jani away from her.

Jani cried out as she fell backwards.

Linda lost her balance and tried to grab onto the wooden balcony railing to catch herself. She missed.

Everything seemed to happen so fast and also in slow motion at the same time. Tyler leapt forward to try and grab Linda but her short, tight top gave nothing to hold onto. She flipped over the railing, literally head over heels and landed in the grass below. The porch was easily four feet off the ground.

Linda swore and then cried out.

Aileen ran over to Jani, terrified Linda's weapon-like shoe had stabbed her in the belly. "Are you okay?"

"Yeah, just landed on my ass real hard. If my legs weren't so freakin' skinny I'd have some fat on my ass to absorb the landing." She grabbed Aileen's hand and pulled herself up. "Where's Linda?"

Tyler had hurdled over the balcony. "She's down here."

Jani and Aileen rushed down the porch to the stairs near the back of the house.

Tyler crouched beside Linda who lay spread out on her back. "I think she's okay. Just really drunk still."

Jani plugged her nose. "At least she managed to avoid landing in her puke."

Aileen squinted and pointed to Linda's arm tucked grotesquely under her. "I think her arm's broken."

"Oh shit!" Tyler shook his head. "I was so freakin' concerned about her head, neck, back and legs, I didn't even look." He rubbed his face with his hands. "We need to get her to a hospital."

"Let me go grab my car. Aileen and I can take her," Jani grabbed her keys out of her pocket.

"I'll come," Tyler insisted.

"You can't leave the party. Don't tell anyone. We're so dead if Coach finds out," Jani covered her mouth with her hand.

"Guys, I'm fine." Linda sat up and stared at her left shoulder. "Freakin' cool! What this!" She shook her shoulder as her left arm flapped helplessly.

"Her arm's not broken. She dislocated her shoulder." Tyler knelt down beside Linda. "You're going to be okay. Luckily you're drunk so I'm guessing it doesn't hurt too bad?"

She nodded and gagged. "I think I have to throw up again." She leaned over to her right and sure enough, tossed more disgusting purple liquid. "I'm never drinking again."

"Go get your car," Tyler said to Jani. "Both of you go get it. I'll carry her to the front by the road and help you get her in the car."

Aileen forced out a breath she didn't realize she had been holding.

"You okay?"

"Sure." The concern on Tyler's face reminded her how only a few moments earlier his lips had been brushing against hers. She straightened. Now was *not* the time to be thinking about that.

Chapter 10

Jani slammed on her breaks as she stopped in front of the emergency doors of Scott Thompson Hospital. Aileen sat in the back, close by Linda who, thankfully, hadn't thrown up again. Her face had gone quite pale as they rushed to the hospital, but she hadn't cried or moaned once. She was pretty tough, Aileen had to give her that.

"Should we have called nine-one-one?" she asked Jani.

"No. If we can avoid Coach Anderson or Maves finding out, it'll be way easier. For everybody." She jumped out of the car and ran inside, returning a moment later with a nurse pushing a wheelchair.

The nurse helped Linda out of the car and into the chair. "Bit of a crazy night, girls?" she asked. She looked at both of them. "Have either of you two been drinking?"

"No! Honestly." Jani pointed to Linda. "I think she had enough for the three of us."

The nurse scrunched her nose. "And then some."

Aileen and Jani followed the nurse. Jani answered questions as the nurse asked. She handed Jani a clip board to fill out whatever she could for Linda.

Aileen sat down in a waiting chair, while Jani went into a cubicle the nurse closed off with curtains. A doctor with short, dark, slightly mussed brown hair, bright blue eyes and in need of a shave came by and slipped into the curtained room.

Aileen heard Linda cry out as the doctor set her shoulder back in place. The doctor reappeared a moment later from the curtains with the nurse. He filled in a prescription and handed it to the nurse.

Just as Aileen felt herself begin to nod off, Jani tapped her on the shoulder. "Ready to go?"

Aileen blinked and tried to focus. "Linda okay?"

"She's in the car. She'll be fine. That sexy Dr. Bennet fixed her shoulder. He says she's going to have one hell of a hangover but her shoulder is fine. It'll feel bruised but apparently Linda's had it happen a lot. I guess when she was a kid she dislocated it with swimming or something and it slips out pretty easy." They began walking to the car. "Sorry about all of this." Jani walked beside Aileen, her head down. "This isn't exactly the kind of thing that makes you want to come to a university."

Amazingly, Aileen didn't care. She was sure when she got back to Ohio she'd reconsider but the moment before crazy Linda had appeared kept replaying in her mind. The way Tyler had looked at her, the feel of his lips against hers, the way her skin tingled when he touched her. She couldn't seem to get that out of her mind.

"Is it okay you don't mention this to Coach?" Jani asked. "I know it's a lot to ask."

"I won't say a thing. You have my word." They had reached the car where Linda lay in the back seat.

Jani hugged her. "Thanks. I know you probably aren't coming here, but if you do I'd love to be roomies with you. We'll kick ol' Linda out." She shook her head annoyed at her roommate.

"I heard that." Linda mumbled from inside the car, her eyes still closed. "She can have my room if she comes. I'll move downstairs. I promise to NEVER drink again."

Jani rolled her eyes. "I've heard that one before." She unlocked Aileen's door. "Come on, let's get you back to the hotel."

They drove back to UofG in silence.

At the hotel Aileen said good bye to the Jani and Linda. She went straight to her room, changed and crawled into bed. She felt exhausted. As she drifted off, she pictured Tyler kissing her and wondered if she would see him again the next day before she left.

Probably not. The only happy thought she had was that she would see him again that summer at Nationals.

Coach Anderson picked her up and took her out to breakfast at a very nice restaurant. It wasn't in College Corner, but on the other wide of campus. On the way, they drove toward Tyler's house and for a moment Aileen thought they might be picking him up to join them for breakfast. She didn't expect Coach Anderson to, especially because he probably knew about the party the night before, but she was worried about getting in trouble somehow. However, she need not have worried. They passed Tyler's house and kept going until they reached a quaint little restaurant with a cheerful milkmaid on the sign. The outside looked like a hole-in-the-wall style eatery, but the inside was fairly posh.

They settled into a round table with a window overlooking a golf course. It was an all-you-can-eat breakfast buffet with a chef in a high hat making omelets. They smelled heavenly.

Coach Anderson set his briefcase down and tucked his phone into the breast pocket of his shirt. "You hungry?"

She smiled. "Always."

They went over to the omelet bar and she ordered everything on it: mushrooms, onions, ham, sausage, peppers, and cheese. Her flight left late that afternoon, but the shuttle would be leaving close to lunch and she figured this would be her last meal till the airport. She didn't plan on wasting it.

The chef cooked the omelet from scratch and ten minutes later Aileen and Coach Anderson were sitting back at their table.

"Did you enjoy your weekend?" he asked her as they ate.

She nodded and wiped her mouth with a cloth napkin. "I did. I really enjoyed it." *Especially kissing your hurdler.*

"That's good to hear. Do you have any questions about the program or the school?"

Can I see Tyler one more time before I leave? She tried to think of something good to ask. She shook her head, unable to come up with anything because images and thoughts of Tyler kept her brain from thinking clearly. She wanted to see him so bad but knew that wasn't going to happen. She wished she had said goodbye to him last night. She hadn't even gotten to do that.

Coach Anderson reached for his briefcase. He pulled out papers and set them in front of Aileen so she could read them. "I've had a National Letter of Intent drawn up for you." He moved his empty plate and folded his hands on the table. "You don't need to sign this now. That's not our intention. We want you to think about where you want to go and weigh all your options. We hope you chose University of Gatica, but understand you have to go where it is best for you. If you did come here, it would be on a full scholarship. Your school, books, living, everything would be included. You would make a great addition to the team and would fit in perfectly. That would be up to five years of schooling and competing." He tapped his thumbs together. "It's renewed every year but, between me and you, I can promise you we would never change the amount of your scholarship."

Full scholarship. Those were big words. She had been offered a full ride to Stanford, and the other three universities she had visited. Each time the offer on the table surprised her. These coaches were putting a lot of faith in one fast race she had done. It seemed crazy.

"Do I need to decide today?"

Coach Anderson shook his head. "This letter," he tapped the paper sitting on the table, "expires in seventy-hours. If you wanted to sign it now, I wouldn't stop you." He smiled. "However, I think you would prefer to take it home with you.

THE RECRUITING TRIP

Talk it over with your parents. Your coach. This letter expires on February fifteenth."

Aileen picked up the contract. That's really what it was. A contract between her and the University of Gatica.

"If the fifteenth date passes and you are still unsure of where you want to go, I'll continue to stay in contact with you. I'd love to hear how your outdoor season goes. I know you mentioned you wouldn't be competing indoors."

"I wish I was, but my coach thought it was better for me to rest up. I haven't really done a lot of indoor meets." A thought occurred to her. "I have a question. If I signed with Gatica, would you stay in contact with my high school coach? Do you then make up my workouts or does he? Or do you guys work together?"

"What would you want to do?"

He was smart. He was giving her the opportunity to decide. She appreciated it. "I think I would want to try the program. You don't know what you can do unless you step outside of your comfort zone."

"Well said." Coach Anderson smiled. "Most of the athletes here like my sprint and hurdle program. You are welcome to stay in touch with your high school coach and I could send him copies of your workouts if you wanted me to."

She flipped through the Letter of Intent, surprised at the numbers, and so glad she wasn't going to be borrowing money from the government to pay for school. "Is there a date you need to know my decision by?" She understood that the school had other athletes they wanted and they couldn't hold a full scholarship offer forever.

He chuckled. "I'd love to know what you are thinking right now, but it's none of my business. Take the Letter with you and read it over on the plane ride home. We will wait as long as it takes you. I'm willing to risk holding the scholarship. You are worth it."

Wow. Aileen didn't know how to respond.

As Coach Anderson drove her back to the hotel, he chatted about anything and everything that had nothing to do with track or school. He got out of the car, shook her hand. "Have a safe trip back. I'll call you on Monday if that's alright with you. Thanks again for choosing Gatica as one of your visits."

Aileen watched him drive off, the sun shining bright against the melting snow. She sighed and turned to go back to her room to pack. Maybe she would call Becky. She had close to three hours before the shuttle would arrive to take her to the airport. She started to walk towards her door, but was pulled up short by the sight before her.

Chapter 11

Tyler stood in the doorway, his hands pressing against both sides of the door frame, and a coy – almost anxious - grin on his face. "I know you'll be on your way to the airport soon..."

Aileen smiled, kind of enjoying his nervousness. It didn't seem like something he had to deal with very often. "Yes?"

"I heard that Linda's okay." He tapped a fist lightly against the wood frame, as if trying to figure out what to say next. "I'm sure you are, uh, you have a lot of great universities to choose from. I get that. I imagine you are leaning toward Stanford." He tapped against the door frame again, leaning toward her. His chest muscles tightened and his biceps curved as he held his body just out of her reach.

A stirring deep inside her belly swirled. It made her knees weak and her breath disappear. She shouldn't, but she desperately wanted to hold onto the feeling. She tried to concentrate on his face as he spoke.

He chuckled and flashed her a delicious grin. "Anyways, I just came by to tell you that I get it. It's a hard decision to make. I hope you chose Gatica, but I totally understand if you don't."

"There are a lot of offers and things to weigh and compare." She dropped her head forward to steal a shy look through her eyelashes. "I appreciate you coming by."

"Me, too," he whispered. His smile disappeared as his face turned a different kind of serious. The kind of look one had when they really wanted to say or do something to somebody... like kiss them. "You can probably do better than here."

His eyes never left hers.

A boldness blossomed inside of her. She heard his words but read them as something different. *You can do better than me.* That's what he meant. She took a step back into the hotel room. "We can do better than here." She held the door open and bit her lower lip when he froze momentarily in surprise.

Tyler's eyes flitted from her to the bed behind her and instantly back to her face.

She wasn't that kind of girl. She didn't know what had happened to her that weekend, but she knew she wasn't leaving Gatica until Tyler did something to stop the craving inside her. He was the only one who could do that.

His tongue ran over his lips and his eyes burned with desire. Silently he stepped into the room, his face inches from hers, except, he did not kiss her.

It drove Aileen crazy but she played along with him, watching his every move as she stepped back and leaned against the wall. She knew she had a cocky grin on her face. She couldn't stop it. It was apparent that he hadn't been expecting anything so bold from her. Neither had she. However, he obviously felt the connection she had noticed from the first time they talked at the indoor track. The feeling had obviously been mutual.

He pushed the door closed with his foot and pressed his strong hands on the wall behind her as he watched her. Slowly he slid them down and spread his fingers along her ribs and held her.

It took everything she had not to close her eyes and simply surrender to the feeling. She nearly did when he leaned in again, his breath hot against her skin as he continued to hold her gaze, his lips millimeters from her mouth then drifting to her neck.

Yet he still didn't kiss her. He brought his hands lower to her hips and lifted her.

Instinctively her legs wrapped around him as he carried her to the leather couch and set her down. Her fingers trailed down his toned triceps and curled around his elbows. Just when she felt he was finally going to kiss her, he pulled back and sat on the coffee table. His chest heaved, but he did not say anything.

Aileen's body followed him as if connected by a string. She leaned toward him and then hesitated. She sat up, and stared openly at him. She realized he wasn't going to make the first move. He wanted to, but was making the decision completely hers. As she watched him, she pulled her button up shirt off, only her thin black tank top still on.

As her breath came out in small gasps, she gave up trying to reason with her brain. Some things did not require thinking. She pushed off the couch and straddled him on the coffee table, pressing her lips hungrily onto his.

He reached for her, one hand spreading against the small of her back, the other into her hair with curling fingers. She wrapped her arms around his strong shoulders and pulled her tight against him. The thick short hair at the nape of his neck tickled her arm and she had to run her fingers through it.

His face had just a touch of stubble above and below his lips that brushed and seductively scratched against her skin. The slight roughness excited her, offering a hint of something she wasn't used to. He was a junior in university, three years older than her! His tongue slipped inside of her mouth and became her undoing. She had believed it was his eyes which captivated her, but that sexy mouth held a power she begged to be possessed by.

Her body pressed harder against him, unable to get close enough. No one had ever made her feel like this before; excited, terrified, on fire and frozen at the same time. She never wanted the feeling to end.

"I shouldn't be here," he whispered, pulling slightly away before resting his forehead against hers, "but I couldn't stop myself."

With her finger, she lightly traced his kiss-bruised lips. She had done that to him. "I'm glad you're here."

"But I shouldn't be—"

She cut his words off by pressing her finger against his mouth. Slowly she brought her head towards his and let her finger trail down his chin, his neck and onto his chest where she let her entire hand spread across his tight, strong muscles. His heart thudded under her hand.

Her lips brushed lightly against his, again and then again. "You should leave if you don't want this to go any further."

His shocked expression drew laughter from her. He grinned wickedly. "You blow my mind. One minute I think you're this sweet little thang, then last summer when I watched you race, I figured you for a tiger in a cage just waiting to break out. On the track. I never thought it off the track. You're unbelievably sexy and incredibly graceful. Like a female lioness... or a cheetah. In your walk, the way you attack the hurdles, in the weight room." He groaned. "You could be my worst distraction."

She had never thought of herself as a sexy. She closed her mouth when she realized it had fallen opened.

He brushed a lock of her hair away from her face and twirled it between his fingers before gently tucking it behind her ear. "I know you're pretty set on going to Stanford. I don't blame you. However, I promise I'll do my best to show you the ropes here at U of G if you came. Gatica has some things Stanford will never have."

"Are you offering to take me under your wing?" Somewhere in the back of her brain, a thought ran through, *Is he here to get me to sign for the school or because he wants me here **with** him?*

He flashed her a sexy smile. "I'll gladly offer my body and skills."

Her eyebrows rose. "Really?"

"Whatever it takes. Wouldn't it rock to have two NCAA champions, in the same event?" His hands ran expertly down her back and up again, tracing her rib cage and making her body want to press tight up against him.

She entwined her fingers together on his neck. Still sitting straddled against him she squeezed her thighs ever-so-slightly so her hips edged closer against him. A hardness teased against her inner thigh. She knew exactly what it was. "Can I let you in on a little secret?" She brushed her lips against his ear, letting her hot breath tease his neck. "I don't like losing, either."

Postlude

UNIVERSITY OF GATICA

Athletic Letter of Intent/Scholarship Offer

The following terms and conditions define an offer of an athletic scholarship for participation in the sport of track and field by University of Gatica and the acceptance of that scholarship by <u>Aileen Nessa</u> for the 2016-17 academic year.

I. AMOUNT OF OFFER:

This offer is a scholarship in the amount of $ 18,500.00 which is equivalent to 100% of the tuition cost for the 2016-2017 academic year and living expenses; $ 5,564.00 will be applied to the Fall 2016 semester and $ 5,564.00 will be applied to the Spring 2017 semester. $7,372.00 will be applied to living expenses for the 2016-2017 academic year.

II. QUALIFICATION FOR ATHLETIC SCHOLARSHIP

THE RECRUITING TRIP

1. The student-athlete must be eligible to participate in intercollegiate athletics upon enrollment at University of Gatica according to the Constitution and By-Laws of the National Collegiate Athletic Association (NCAA). Signing of this letter indicates intent only and does not guarantee admission to the College and/or eligibility to participate. If either condition is not met, both parties agree to void the agreement.

2. The student-athlete agrees to follow all rules and regulations established by the college for students as detailed in the Student Handbook and shall sign a supplementary agreement as required by the Dean of Enrollment Services.

3. The student-athlete further agrees to follow all rules for participation in the scholarship sport as determined by the head coach. These rules include, but are not limited to:

A. The student-athlete will not use drugs, alcohol or tobacco, at any time, while under contract.

B. The student-athlete will not use expletive, offensive or derogatory language at any time.

C. Physical or verbal acts of intimidation or violence by the student-athlete will not be tolerated.

D. All team members are required to attend team meetings, functions, practices, games and road trips—arriving on time for each. Student-athletes are excused from class only to participate in regularly scheduled games. Every effort will be made to schedule practices and team functions so that they do not interfere with class meetings.

E. All team members will be expected to participate in team community service projects and to work on team fund-raising events.

4. The student shall obey all federal, state and local laws and ordinances.

5. Participation in a sport other than the scholarship sport is at the discretion of the head coach of the scholarship sport.

III. CONTINUANCE AND/OR DISCONTINUANCE OF SCHOLARSHIP

1. The student-athlete shall not have his/her scholarship discontinued prior to the end of the academic year for poor athletic performance.

2. The student-athlete shall not have his/her scholarship discontinued prior to the end of the academic year if the student is prevented from participating in the scholarship sport because of illness, injury or other genuine emergency.

3. The student-athlete may have his/her scholarship discontinued immediately if he/she becomes academically ineligible to participate in athletics or the scholarship sport according to the NCAA. The student should familiarize him/herself with these regulations.

4. The student-athlete may have his/her scholarship discontinued immediately if he/she voluntarily withdraws from the team or is dismissed from the team for just cause. To emphasize: Being removed from the team for lack of playing ability does not constitute just cause.

5. The student-athlete may have his/her scholarship discontinued immediately if he/she breaks any of the terms of this agreement; is convicted of violating federal, state or local law other than a minor traffic offense; is found to have violated the rules established for the conduct of students at large at Smith University as detailed in the Student Handbook or breaks any of the rules established by the head coach of the scholarship sport.

6. The student-athlete may have his/her scholarship discontinued immediately if he/she is discovered to have fraudulently misrepresented prior academic records or any other information requested during the admissions and/or financial aid process.

7. Discontinuance of the scholarship would mean the student-athlete would immediately be responsible for paying prorated balances which may result.

8. This scholarship is granted for the 2016-2017 academic year only. The student-athlete must agree to attend both the Fall and Spring semester regardless of what semester the sport is played. Continuance beyond the Spring 2017 semester is at the discretion of the college and/or head coach.

9. This offer does not guarantee a roster spot on the University of Gatica Track and Field team. The student-athlete shall not have his/her scholarship discontinued in the event the student-athlete does not make the final active roster.

This document represents an offer regarding only an athletic scholarship between University of Gatica and the student-athlete. The scholarship must be confirmed by an official award letter from the Financial Aid Office after completion of all documents required by the college. All University of Gatica Scholarships require a semester and cumulative grade-point average (GPA) of 2.0. Student-athletes who fail to maintain these grading standards will have their scholarships terminated at the end of the term in which they fell below the standards.

IV. APPEAL OF DISCONTINUANCE

1. Discontinuance of scholarship for cause prior to the end of the 2016-2017 academic year may be appealed by the student. A committee consisting of the Faculty Athletic Representative, the Director of Athletics, Director of Financial Aid and the Dean of Enrollment Services shall consider the appeal. If any member of this committee is unavailable or disqualifies him/herself from hearing an appeal, the Dean of Enrollment Services shall appoint a replacement to the committee. If the Dean of Enrollment Services is not able to head the appeal, the President of the College shall appoint his/her replacement.

VI. DECLARATION OF INTENT:

By signing below, I agree to attend University of Gatica during the 2016-2017 academic year and to participate on the college's intercollegiate team in the scholarship sport specified on page 1 of this agreement. I have read each of the forgoing conditions and understand each. I agree to abide by the conditions and to represent the college in a positive manner. I understand that if this letter is not signed and returned to the Head Track and Field Coach by June 5, 2016 University of Gatica may elect to withdraw its offer:

__Aileen Nessa February 14, '16
   Name (Aileen Nessa)
   Signature   Date

As representatives of University of Gatica, the undersigned agree to offer the Athletic Scholarship described to the above named student for the 2016-2017 academic year under the agreed-upon conditions.

  _Coach Anderson__   Feb 12, 2016
   Head Coach
  ___*AJ Wright*_____*Feb 10, 2016*
   Director of Athletics
  ____Dean Willows_____Feb 10, 2016
   Dean of Enrollment Services

THE END
Of
The Recruiting Trip
STRONGER,
Book II of
The University of Gatica Series
COMING SOON!

Find out what happens with Tyler and Aileen in
FASTER

Hope you enjoyed
THE RECRUITING TRIP.
If you have a moment, it would be greatly appreciated if you could leave a sentence or two review so others can also find the series to read and enjoy!

Thanks, Lexy Timms

If you enjoyed The Recruiting Trip, try Lexy Timm's Saving Forever Series:

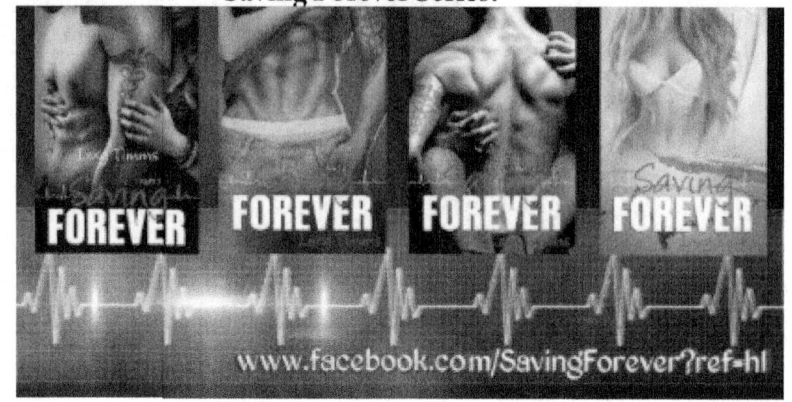

SAVING FOREVER SERIES
Book Trailer:
http://www.youtube.com/watch?v=ABs_uaeEamo
Website: https://www.facebook.com/SavingForever

EXCERPT INCLUDED!

Saving Forever

Chapter 1

"You do realize you have a very unique name for the business you're in?" The doctor smiled and winked at her. His hazelnut eyes sparkled with mischief. "I'm sure you've been told that a million times."

Charity laughed. "My mother must have planned it all while I was in her tummy." She tucked a chunk of her long blond hair behind her ear. It had been six years since her mother had lost her battle against cancer, which had completely changed Charity's career course. The day after the funeral, she had dropped out of medical school and hadn't looked back since. She couldn't say the same about her father. She forced a grin and focused on the moment. "It's even more ironic now that I'm signing a two-year contract with you guys. How shall we put the press release? Forever Hope Hospital hires Charity Thompson as their new Fundraiser Liaison. Kind of a tongue twister, eh, Dr. Parker?"

"Just Malcolm, please. We're working together now. It's in the two-year contract you just signed. It says you are to refer to Dr. Parker as Malcolm only." He held it up, teasing her.

Dr. Parker—er, Malcolm—couldn't be much older than Charity, maybe five years tops. Cropped hair and chiselled features probably made him popular talk amongst the staff and patients. She knew he was single, recently divorced, with no children. She wondered how long it would take a first year or nurse to 'make the rounds' with him. Or maybe he would surprise her and actually be a decent guy.

"As for the press release, I can't wait to see everyone and anyone's reaction. It's going to be a big success. Between the humor in your name and job, your awesome track record for success..." He pointed and in a very kind voice added, "Your beautiful face, plus the fact that your father is *the* Doctor Thompson, I'm not sure we should send the press release to the local papers or to the American Journal of Medicine." He stood and reached out his hand. "I'm teasing again, of course. We're all very excited to have you on board."

Charity stood and shook his hand, making sure to add just the right about of firmness to show her strength and still remain feminine. "I'm excited to get started."

"This hospital needs your help. We're in dire straights. Between the state cutbacks, the simple lack of funds, our long term care ward, and our outpatient surgery floor is anciently outdated, we either need to update or close down. People are starting to skip past us and are driving the extra forty-five minutes to Atlanta General." He shook his head. "You already know this, sorry. I just hear it everyday, a million times a day."

Charity sat back down and pulled her iPad out of her briefcase. "Then we need to get started right away." She flipped to the screen she'd written the list of things she needed from the hospital. "I'm going to need the hospital's financial records, and a calendar of events you already have set up. I'd like to plan a charity luncheon in about six weeks to get the ball rolling. Remember, this isn't going to be fixed overnight. It's a process and two years is the goal. We'll get there."

Vibration from the doctor's cell phone on his desk made her pause. They both looked at the phone and then at each other.

"Continue, please." He glanced at the phone and then back at her.

"You're busy. You need to take care of hospital issues. Why don't I talk to your assistant and check your calendar? We need to pick a day in five or six weeks that you can take a long lunch break." She thought back to his comment about her having a pretty face. "We need to use those good looks of yours and get some lovely high society ladies wanting to spend money on the hospital with the hot doc."

He blinked, surprise clear on his face. "I'm not sure if I should be insulted or pleased. Hot doc?"

She laughed. "Sometimes pretty works and you have to use it." She stood and slipped her briefcase strap over her shoulder. "Sorry, doc, but you're single, good-looking, and funny. I'm going to have to use you as a marketing tool to get a few charities going." She held up her hand. "I promise no cheesy date auctions or prostitution. Just need to use your... your atmosphere to see how awesome the staff and hospital really is."

"I'll do whatever it takes. I love this place and want everyone else to love it as well."

They were going to work together just fine. "You need to go be a doctor and I need to set up my office."

The doctor slapped his forehead. "I almost forgot! Your new office is to the right of the elevator. I've had it cleared and your name's supposed to be up on the glass by the end of the day. I'll get my assistant to show you where and she'll also bring any information you need." He pressed the red button on the intercom phone on his desk. "Amanda, do you mind helping Ms. Thompson?"

A millisecond later, the office door opened and in rushed a tiny, petite lady. Her silver hair in a messy bun held a pair of reading classes stuck on the top of her head. "Doctor Parker, Doctor Mallone is trying to get a hold of you. He needs you in emerg right away." She turned, almost floating like a little fairy. "Ms. Thompson, let's go." She disappeared out the door, her little shoes tapping down the hall.

It felt like being in third grade all over again. Charity raised her eyebrows but wasn't about to disobey Amanda. As she took a step toward the door, a smooth hand touched her elbow.

"She's harmless," Malcolm whispered, his warm breath tickling her ear, "but I've never crossed her." He chuckled as he let go of her. "Good luck."

Charity mouthed a sarcastic *Thank-you* and hurried out the door. She could feel Malcolm's breath cooling on her skin as her long strides slowly caught up to Amanda.

"I had a two-sided desk set up in your office. I also had them set up a bookcase, but didn't know what else you would need." Amanda's words punched out with each tap of her shoes. She stopped in front of a frosted glass door and pulled a key out of her pocket. "This is yours." She handed to key to Charity. "I'm glad you've come. Welcome to Forever Hope. Just let me know if you need anything else." She stood waiting.

"Thanks." Charity realized the woman wanted her to open the door so she hurriedly put the key into the lock and turned it. She pushed the door open and grinned when she stepped inside.

"Will it work?" Amanda asked.

The office was actually two rooms, kind of like a waiting room and then an archway that showed a glimpse of a large, light wood stained two-sided desk. The walls were completely bare except for a fresh coat of pale yellow paint. *Bright without feeling like a hospital.* It gave her an idea. "It's going to be perfect!"

"Lovely. I'm down the hall if you need me." Amanda disappeared out the door.

Charity set her briefcase against the wall by the door and pressed her lips together. She'd done six large-figure multi-million dollar fundraisers but never had an office like this. *Two rooms!*

Racing through the brightly painted white arch, she surveyed the second room. It was a bit smaller than the first room, but both had large window panels to look over the city. Day or night, the view was probably amazing. The two-sided desk had a brand new computer still in its box sitting on the far side, along with a phone already set up. The leather chair behind seemed to beg her to try it out. Well, she couldn't disappoint it.

The soft leather felt perfect under her. She tested out the wheels and tried sliding from one side of the desk to the other. No problem. She slipped her heels off and felt the wood floor against her bare feet. It made her want to dance. *Focus, Charity.*

She pushed her chair away from the desk and went back to the first room to look around. The bright, empty room would make a perfect conference room. Give it a laid back, homey atmosphere and possibly donors would relax the minute they stepped in. She pulled her Blackberry out of the short-sleeved red jacket that went with her black dress.

Maybe a loveseat, definitely a round table, four comfortable chairs, two ottomans, plant, fridge, cabinet to hold glasses, wine rack.

She glanced around. There were three walls to work with since she didn't want to put anything but a low table near the windows. If she painted the one wall with chalk paint, that would be a perfect note-board and would also work as a projector screen for presentations.

A buzzing in her hand caught her attention. She had a call. Quickly saving the shopping list, she then switched screens to check the caller ID. She almost dropped the phone when she saw the number.

Chapter 2

"Dad!" Her father never rang unless there was an emergency. "Is everything all right?"

"Hullo?" The voice that answered wasn't her father's. It was husky, with a clear accent.

It took her by surprise and sent a shiver down her spine at the same time.

"I'm sorry, is this Charity?"

She scratched her head, trying to recognize the caller. Australian accent? Or New Zealand? "Where's my father?"

"I'm not too sure, actually." The stranger chuckled. "I was just in a meeting with him an' he said he needed to call you. Suddenly he tosses me the phone and rushes off to some code three over the intercom." A slight grating noise echoed through the phone like the stranger was rubbing a five o'clock shadow. "I'm sorry. I don't even know what he wanted to tell you."

"That's okay. He does have a habit of rushing off to save the day. Who is this, by the way?"

"I'm Elijah."

"Hi Elijah, I'm Charity." She shook her head. Was she honestly flirting with some stranger over the phone? Her father's phone on top of it. She really needed to get out more.

"It's a pleasure to meet you." He chuckled. "Well, over the phone anyway."

She smiled. "Not to make you the messenger, but you can let my dad know I've arrived and he can call me when he has a free moment."

"Arrived?"

She absently waved her hand in the air and walked around the room surveying what she needed to do first. Hardware store, the furniture store. "I just started a new contract down here in Atlanta."

"A little warmer than New York at the moment."

"Definitely."

Muffled voices carried over the phone. "I apologize again," Elijah said, "but Dr. Thompson needs me."

"No problem. Have a great afternoon."

"You too."

Charity slipped her phone into her jacket pocket and grabbed her briefcase. She wondered what Elijah looked like. That sexy accent surely belonged to a good looking guy. She rolled her eyes. The guy was over a thousand miles away and she had a new job with a lot of work to do.

Speaking of work. She needed to get a list of past donators, skim through the local papers to find the elite social class. The first group would be women. Doctors' wives and local celebrities. She already had connections to a couple of popular bands that would do charity concerts for her. It was simply a matter of getting dates and plans to coincide.

She headed out of the office and back down the hall to Amanda's office.

Amanda sat behind her computer, reading glasses on the bridge of her nose. She smiled at Charity. "What do you need, sweetie?"

Charity dropped into the chair in front of Amanda's desk. "I need lists. People who have donated to the hospital, anyone big named or wealthy who have been here. Even those who wished to remain discreet. I'll contact them on the down-low but I need names." She went through her mental list of things she wouldn't have access to find. "Has the board made blueprints or hired architecture to design the new wing Malcolm wants to add?"

Amanda shook her head. "I don't believe they have." Her hand slid her computer mouse around and she clicked it a bunch of times. Pages started printing out of the massive computer behind her. "Dr. Parker started collecting data when he was pretty sure you would agree to help us out."

The printer continued printing out page after page after page. That was a good sign. More meant a lot of options and possibilities. "Has Malc—Dr. Parker or any other doctor worked on athletes as well? Anyone from the Braves, or Hawks or the Falcons?"

"I'm sure there are quite a few."

"Does every doctor have a seat on the board?"

Amanda shook her head. "I don't believe so."

Her father was a stickler for every person having their say. He was adamant about all doctors meeting at least twice a year to discuss hospital issues. His hospital would be a success and never be in need of someone like her. It made her very proud of him.

"We'll need to set up a meeting with everyone." She ignored the slightly annoyed look on Amanda's face. Charity had two years to turn this place into a success story and she needed everyone willing to work with her. She knew what needed to be done and it was never easy at first, but that would change. "How about you send me everyone's email address?"

"You can't get everyone to meet at the same time. The hospital would have to close for the day."

Charity smiled. She knew better than to argue. "You're right. I'll have to come up with something that works for everyone." She stood and checked her watch. "I've got errands to run for my office that I want to do tomorrow, and my stuff is supposed to be delivered to my apartment sometime after five today. Gotta jet."

Amanda scooted her chair back and grabbed the massive stack of printed paper. "Do you want me to bind these for you?"

"That would be awesome. I'll start going through them tomorrow then."

"Good luck."

"Thanks. I think I'm going to need it."

"And Charity?" Amanda set her glasses on the top of her head.

"Yes?"

"I'm glad you here."

Amanda was full of surprises. Charity grinned. "Me, too."

Chapter 3

Trying to balance her groceries and case of water in one hand, Charity slipped the key into her apartment door with the other. She had met the moving company earlier. It hadn't taken long to unpack, and all that was left were five clothing suitcases in her bedroom. She then ran out to grab food for dinner and breakfast in the morning.

She kicked the door shut with her foot and glanced around. It was a studio apartment with a double sized living room, which opened to a modern kitchen. Light grey stained wood covered the floors and the two rooms were painted a soft white.

Very bright. And very empty.

That had been done on purpose. A leather antique psychologist couch was set against the far wall, mirrors covered another wall, and a high tech stereo system took up most of the space on the last wall. The only remaining wall had windows and a door to a simple balcony.

Charity slipped off her shoes and padded on bare feet to the kitchen. She set the case of water down on the breakfast bar and quickly put away the groceries. Before putting the water under the table, she grabbed the remote beside the case and turned the stereo on. The tall speakers came to life and Charity reached for a bottle from the case. As she strolled to her bedroom, her fingers tapped the music's beat against the plastic water container. By the time she reached her room, she was full-out dancing.

She changed into tights and a sport top, then headed back to the living room. She had been dancing since she was six. Her mom had encouraged her to try every form of dance and she loved them all. Somehow, all the different types of dancing had rolled into her own artistic interpretation and she was phenomenal at it, but very few people knew. It came in handy during the galas and dinners if someone asked her to dance and she could surprise guests.

Dancing was her workout, her stress reducer, her fun time and her down time.

An hour and a shower later, she started cooking dinner. Munching on a carrot, the little red light flashing on the phone caught her attention. She flipped her screen on and saw several emails from Amanda with attachments, an email confirming the paint and furniture for her office would be delivered in the morning, and her father had called about ten minutes prior.

He hadn't left a message so she pressed the button to call him, putting him on speaker so she could continue cutting vegetables.

"Dr. Thompson."

"Dad, it's me." Charity tried not to roll her eyes. He had caller ID so he knew it was her.

"Charity. How can I help you?"

She shook her head. "You phoned me earlier and tried again a bit ago. I was in the shower and just saw the missed call. I assume you wanted to talk to me." No 'how are you doing?' or 'how's Atlanta?'.

"Oh yes. I did. I was going to have my secretary call but I knew you'd say no if she asked."

Charity set the knife down. She didn't want to stab her phone. "Nice, Dad. I really appreciate you starting a phone conversation on the negative. Why don't you just ask me what you need and I'll let you know what I think?"

"Fine. I'm turning sixty-five next year." He paused.

"I know." A strange thought crossed her mind. She never assumed he would, but what if... "Are you retiring?"

"Hell no! I'm more than competent as a doctor, probably still better than most of the doctors I know."

No lie there. He was one of the best doctors in the country, even had a hospital named after him. "I didn't think you would, but why the phone call just over six months before your birthday?"

"The hospital wants to make a big deal with it. I guess they need to. I said I would take care of it since I don't want it to be about me. I want the focus on something else."

She had no idea where he was going with this.

"I was wondering..." He swallowed and a quick sigh echoed through the phone. "We'd like to hire you to do the party."

She blinked in surprise. He hated her job and always made sure she knew how disappointed he was that she'd dropped out of med school. "I'm not a party planner."

"You don't organize parties and plan big events?"

Good point. "I do but they are for hospitals wings, additions, equipment. The galas are to raise money for non-profit issues hospitals need." Not some retirement party where the birthday dude wasn't even retiring.

"Exactly. That's what I—what we want to hire your for. To make money for some new equipment at the hospital. My milestone age marker is just the excuse to do it."

Charity tapped her fingers against her lip as she thought. It was actually a very good idea. Everyone knew and liked her father. He never made a fuss about himself publicly so a lot of doctors from all over the country would fly in for the night. Plus the countless patients whose lives he had saved. It was a great idea.

So why her?

"I've just signed a two year contract down here in Atlanta. I can't drop everything for them for six months and help you. That wouldn't be fair."

"I'm not expecting anything spectacular. It's fine. I'm sorry I bothered you."

THE RECRUITING TRIP

Giving up that easy? That wasn't her father. That competitive side of her kicked in. He didn't think she could do spectacular? Boy was he in for a surprise. "How much money are you hoping to raise?"

"It doesn't matter."

"How much?"

"A hundred thousand would cover half the price of the equipment in the emergency room."

"Your gala could easily raise quadruple that."

He scoffed. "Really?"

"Easy." She thought about going back home. Did she want to? Part of her did. The kid in her wanted to prove to her father that she was good at her job. That she deserved to be patted on the head and told she'd done a good job. That her career change hadn't been a bad choice. "Look. If you can handle working on the weekends for this, I can do it. The flight to NY from Atlanta is direct. It's only a one night gala. I can work online from here and fly up twice a month or whatever to get it set there." Six months wasn't that long.

"You'll do it?" The surprise in his voice made her smile.

"Sure. I'll have to come up this weekend to find a location. It's going to be a time crunch, but it'll work."

"Perfect." Scribbling of a pen made its way through the phone. "I need to go. Duty calls."

"Life of a doctor. I'll meet you at the hospital Friday afternoon sometime. I'll email you my flight details."

"I can send someone to pick you up."

"Don't worry. It'll be easier if I rent a car."

"Sounds good." He paused. "And thanks, Charity."

"You're welcome."

She stared at the phone after her father hung up. What had she just gotten herself into?

Chapter 4

Once off the plane Charity waited for her bags and then picked up her rental car. The mid-size car she hired wasn't available so the young teller bumped her up to a Mustang. Blue. Sapphire blue. She laughed out loud in the parking lot when she tossed her suitcase and bag in the trunk. The weekend might actually turn out to be fun.

The week itself had been busy. She'd painted the office, had it decorated, went through the email list, and set up a luncheon with Malcolm for Monday. They needed to go over a few plans and she also needed to meet with the board next week. Juggling the two jobs would be interesting.

She drove straight to the hospital and parked in the visitor parking section. The newly designed hospital almost looked inviting. They had torn down the older hospital two blocks away months ago. The grey outer walls had loads of windows and sections of it spread like rays of sun around the nucleus.

The warm heated air brushed the cold autumn air away as she stepped though the sliding doors. She headed for the elevator but slipped into a restroom just before. She washed her hands and looked in the mirror. Her ponytail had slipped down so she grabbed two chunks of hair to tighten it. The pony band snapped and shot off like an elastic.

"Crap!" Charity searched through her purse for another one but found nothing. She ran her fingers through her hair and tucked a few strands behind an ear. It would have to do. Except now she needed to touch up her makeup. Little makeup worked with a ponytail but not with her hair down. She grabbed a lip gloss and added eyeliner and mascara. She stepped back. Dark jeans and white button up would have to do.

She squared her shoulders and exhaled a long breath. "Please give me patience and don't piss Dad off," she mumbled before leaving the bathroom. She hit the elevator button and the far door slid open. *Perfect timing.*

An older couple walked off together and she smiled at them before stepping into the lift. Leaning against the wall, a tall glass of hot water stood in medical scrubs. Short, dark, slightly mussed brown hair, bright blue eyes, and a sexy five o'clock shadow held Charity's gaze a moment longer than what was considered polite. She quickly turned and pressed the sixth floor button. It was already lit up. Hot muscle guy had to get off on the same floor.

She closed her eyes and silently sighed. She should have looked at his badge instead of his face. The thought of his chest made her wonder what he might look like with his shirt off. She forced herself to open her eyes and stare straight ahead. *You're being ridiculous. Cute guy and you act like a thirteen-year-old boy-crazy kid.*

She turned around and smiled, willing her eyes to stay on his face, not cruise down and then back up. "Are you a doctor here?"

"I am." The stranger smiled but offered no more information.

Sexy smile. She tried again. "Is your office on the sixth floor?"

"It is."

Did she detect an accent? Her eyebrows furrowed together. Had they met before? She would have definitely remembered. She glanced down at his hospital tag just as the elevator came to a stop. *Dr. Bennet.* The door slid open so she turned to step out. She stopped short when she realized she didn't know where to go.

Dr. Bennet walked right into her and grabbed her elbow so she wouldn't fall.

"I'm so sorry. Are you a'right?"

Definitely an Australian accent, or something by there. "It's my fault." She shook her head. "I'm not sure where Dr. Thompson's office is. Last time I was here they were still finishing this floor."

Two young nurses walked by. One winked at the doctor. "Hi, Elijah." The other nurse elbowed her. "Oops. Hello, Doctor Bennet." The two disappeared into the nurse's room.

Elijah? Charity remembered her dad's phone call when she'd spoken to him. "I'm Charity." She held out her hand. "I'm Dr. Thompson's daughter. We spoke earlier this week on the phone."

Elijah reached for her hand. His warm, strong fingers enclosed around hers and he smiled at her again. "I remember. You're much more beautiful in person."

No wonder the nurses were so friendly. He was a lady's man.

"I can take you to your dad. I was just about to see him myself."

"That'd be great." If he was a flirt, she could flirt, too. "Lead the way."

He pulled his phone out of his chest pocket and checked his messages. "I just need to call downstairs to see if my x-rays are done." He headed past the nurses' station and down the hall.

Charity followed and admired his lean muscular shoulders that dipped into a firm derriere that looked fantastic in hospital pants. She felt her cheeks grow warm. *There's nothing wrong with appreciating a fit body. Get over it, girl.*

"...Thanks. Have someone send them up to the sixth floor review room. I need them quick." Elijah tucked his phone back in his pocket. "Sorry about that. So, how long are you in town to see your dad?"

"Just the weekend. He wants a fancy to-do for his sixty-fifth. He's asked me to plan it."

"I'm sure you'll make it amazing." He scratched the stubble on his chin. "I have to admit, I Googled you after we spoke on the phone. You're quite the successful donor-fundraiser... party planner... thing." He shrugged and made a confused face. "I don't know what your official title is."

"Neither does my father," she teased, "but at least he knows what I do or he wouldn't have called." She noticed the wing they'd been walking down now had expensive wooden doors. The first office had her dad's name on the plaque, and across the hall was Elijah's name. "You must be pretty special to have an office right here." *By my dad* is what she wanted to say but held back. Her opinion of her father was not shared with fellow doctors. He was *the* man. The Dr. Scott Thompson. Lifesaver super-hero.

"The chief gets the next best office." Elijah dropped his head a bit and grinned like a little boy. "Sorry, just trying to impress you."

Charity blinked, surprised at his honesty. "I'm impressed. A little." She pretended to shrug. "You're pretty young to be chief. I'd ask who you had to sleep with to get the job, but since my dad's in charge, I don't really want to know."

Elijah's head tilted back and he burst out laughing.

The door to her father's office swung open, probably from the sound in the hallway. "Charity!"

Chapter 5

A bit more grey in his hair and a little more tired, her father still commanded power. Years of hard work and respect earned from success gave him that posture. He was one of the best doctors in the country, even at almost sixty-five. He would always be distinguished and handsome. Charity sometimes wondered why he hadn't remarried since her mom passed away. He'd probably had a lot of offers.

She hadn't seen her dad in over a year, almost two years. Two Christmases ago she had flown home to spend the holidays with him. Christmas day ended in a big row right after they had gone to the gravesite to drop some flowers off on her mother's stone. She'd left early the next morning, not even sure if her father was still in the house or already gone to the hospital. Last year she made up the excuse she had to work so she wouldn't have to fly home. She felt guilty, but guilt was better than fighting with a man who couldn't be wrong.

They still called each other once every two or three weeks and never discussed the fight. He had made the first call and she had called him the next time. It continued until he called earlier this week. Four days and two phone calls had broken the pattern.

"Dad!" She awkwardly stepped forward to shake his hand at the same time he leaned over to hug her.

"I trust your flight was all right?" He stepped back so she could come into his office.

"It was fine." She stepped through, absently tucking a strand of hair behind her ear.

Elijah followed her into the office. She'd momentarily forgotten he had brought her down the hall. "Why don't I let the two of you catch up and I'll chat with you later, Scott."

"No!" both Charity and her father said at the same time.

"I mean," said her father, "I want your opinion on what I'm hiring Charity to do for the hospital. As chief you also need to sign off on it."

Charity glanced back and forth at both men. Did her dad seriously mean that, or was he just as afraid as her to be in the same room alone together?

Elijah checked his watch. "I can really only stay a moment. I have surgery in thirty minutes and need to scrub in with a first year. It's a cardiothoracic, so I'm not leaving my attending in charge."

Her father harrumphed. "Right." He clapped his hands and walked around to his desk and sat down behind it. "Why don't you meet Charity and me for drinks after?" He stared at Charity. "What's that place we went to before... the Threaded Cork? Yes, that's it. Meet us at the Threaded Cork when you are done." It wasn't a request.

Elijah nodded. "Sounds good. You're treating then, right?" By his smile and relaxed stance, it was obvious to Charity that he wasn't intimidated by her father. Elijah just earned a new level of respect from her. He smiled at her, and just as he turned to leave he winked, then strolled out the door.

An uncomfortable silence filled the room after the door closed. Her father cleared his throat as he rested his fingertips against each other. "I really appreciate you being willing to take this on."

"It's not everyday your father turns sixty-five." She crossed her legs and then uncrossed them. "Do you want this gala to be a dinner or just a party?" Part of her dreaded planning it, but another part really wanted to show her father how good she was at her job.

"What do you think?" His thumbs tapped a steady beat while he waited for her answer.

"Well, it all depends on how you want the evening to go. Do you want to focus on raising money for the hospital, or your birthday, or the fact that you're stepping down?"

"I'm not stepping down." He straightened against the back of the chair.

Charity had to make herself resist the urge to let her eyes roll upward to the ceiling. "Okay, but from a professional standpoint, I need to know what the theme is going to be. If I don't ask you and set the wrong theme, you are going to hate it."

"Right. Sorry." He relaxed his straight posture by a tenth of a degree and ran his fingers through his hair. "I built this hospital so we could be a leader in research and innovative surgeries. I plan to keep up the research end and help run the board, but Dr. Bennett is the chief now. He's good at his job." He looked Charity directly in the eye. "Lousy at staying away from the women. Ask the nurses or first years or anyone who seems to look good in a skirt."

Charity burst out laughing. She couldn't help it. "Are you jealous, Dad?"

"Just warning my head-strong daughter."

"And I wonder where I got that from."

"Yes, well okay then." He checked his watch and stood. "I really don't care what you do with the evening. I'd just like the focus to be on the hospital. I figured my sixty-fifth would be a good excuse to throw it. If it makes money, great. If not, that's fine too."

"Sure." She knew what he meant. He wasn't expecting much from her. Well, she would surprise him. Six months to plan it would be tight, but if she flew up two or three weekends a month she could make it a great turnout. "What time do you want to meet at the Threaded Cork?"

"Meet? I just thought we'd drive back to the house together and go from there."

Charity's cheeks grew warm. "I, um, I booked a hotel room. I just thought it'd be easier for me to work and –"

"Right," he cut her off. "I have some work here to do as well. Why don't we aim for six o'clock then?"

"Six o'clock it is. I'll have some ideas and check out some possible venues. We're going to need to pick a spot as soon as we can."

"Perfect." He went to the door and held it open for her. "I'll see you there."

Charity pressed her lips together as she bent to grab her purse. Six months of being uncomfortable seemed like a prison sentence at the moment, but she owed it to her mother to make the effort.

After leaving the office, she took the stairs down to the main floor and let the cool wind soothe her face. Heading to the parking lot, she grinned when she found the Mustang. Maybe a new outfit to go with the car might be something to cheer her up. She could shop and brainstorm at the same time.

Charity turned the blow dryer off as she finished straightening her hair. She'd managed to find a simple black sleeveless dress at Michael Korrs and a pair of black shoes with just the right amount of heel to look sexy without looking like a stripper. She wondered how Elijah would be like outside of the hospital. She mentally kicked the thought out. Tonight's dinner had to do with her father's fundraiser gala. Her dress was fun but also completely business suited. Eye shadow followed by mascara and a dab of lip gloss and she was ready to go.

She stuffed her iPad into her briefcase and her jacket. Its length matched the dress's – perfect without even trying.

Parking downtown turned out to not be as easy. Friday night in a busy city had everyone and their neighbour looking for a parking spot. Charity drove the block around the Threaded Cork three times before getting slightly lucky and spotting a couple getting into their car. She flipped her blinker on and carefully parallel parked the car. Good thing she hadn't gone with the higher heels, as she had a few streets to walk. Tossing her keys into her purse, she stepped out and walked around the car to grab her briefcase.

Someone whistled. "Wow. That's quite the ride."

Elijah. The accent was hard to miss. She smiled, locked the car, and turned around. "Rental place gave it to me. I honestly didn't ask."

"Let me get that for you." He offered his hand and took her briefcase, slinging it over his shoulder. "You must have made quite the impression to the car clerk."

She laughed as they started walking. "He was kinda young. You have to troll around for a parking spot as well?"

"I actually took the subway. Surgery went a bit longer than I thought, so I showered and changed at the hospital."

She glanced down at his outfit from the corner of her eye. Black pants, fitted button up, and she caught a whiff of a delicious men's cologne. "How did the surgery go?"

"Quite well, thank you for asking. The patient is a young woman in her early forties. She had a small hiccup while on the table but we fixed it, and her heart, in the end." He slipped his hands into his pockets.

"You could have stayed at the hospital if you preferred." She said it just to be polite but was more than pleased he had come. Talking to her dad over dinner on her own seemed daunting.

"And miss seeing you dressed to the nines?" He pretended to clutch his heart. "I'll have to get mine checked out when I get back to the hospital."

"You are really, really cheesy." She laughed, despite the corniness.

"A bit too much?" He grinned and small lines crinkled near his eyes. The look was striking.

"It suites you," she replied honestly.

They turned the corner and headed down the last block length to the Threaded Cork.

"So what is it your father wants to hire you to do for the hospital?"

Charity pushed the fallen strap of her purse back on her shoulder. "To be honest, I'm a bit surprised he called me. He doesn't quite agree with my career choice." She waved her hand, embarrassed to be sharing that information with him. "I mean, he's turning sixty-five, and since he is *the* Doctor Scott Thompson, he knows he has to do something big with the ol' milestone number. He'd rather make the emphasis on the hospital than him."

"It's a great idea."

They reached the entrance to the Threaded Cork and Elijah handed Charity her briefcase and then held the door open for her. The outside of the building had not changed since the last time she had come. It had the old heritage appeal but painted with modernist colours and flare.

Dim inside, Tiffany lights hanging above each solid table clearly showed who sat at each location. Her father was already sitting at a place near the far wall. The back of the restaurant where the bar and wine tasting area had been built was quiet. It would fill after the dinner rush.

Charity led the way to the table and Elijah pulled her chair out for her. Surprised, she managed to remember her manners and whispered, "Thanks."

"Did you two drive together?" Her father raised a single eyebrow. How he had ever mastered that ability had always bugged Charity, even as a kid. She tried for hours to make only one brow go up.

"I drove." "I took the subway." Elijah and Charity spoke at the same time and then laughed.

"We met just outside," Charity added.

The waitress came by with three wine glasses and two bottles of wine; one red and one white.

"I took the liberty to order a bottle of each," her father said as he looked at the menu. He smiled at the waitress. "What are your specials tonight?"

After they ordered and filled their wine glasses, Charity pulled a folder out of her briefcase. "I scouted a few places and we have a few options." She flipped her iPad case open and slid through her apps until she found the one she'd set up. Tapping the screen, she slid the tablet so both men could see the hall set up. "I thought about doing the party at the hospital. You have the large gymnasium you could turn into a high school prom setting." She suppressed a giggle when both men's eyebrows mashed together at the same time. "Hey, it may sound cheesy but it would be a huge hit. The entire idea behind prom," she made small circles with her hand, "what happens after prom. You know, the whole package. Laugh all you want, it will get donators giving."

The smirk on Elijah's face told her he liked the idea; the forced smile on her father's told her otherwise.

She slid the tablet picture to another floor diagram. "This is the old downtown concert building. It's heritage but has been completely revamped inside. It's like a Phantom of the Opera kind of building. They have this amazing chandelier that was restored. It sparkles even when the lights are dimmed." She snapped her fingers. "We could make the evening about diamonds. Make it a platinum, gold, and white evening."

Her father topped up Elijah's and his wine glasses. "Quite the opposite of venue ideas."

THE RECRUITING TRIP

"Well, you gave me next to nothing to work with so I'm using every angle to make your evening something you want." She took a long sip of her red wine, embarrassed at her response and that her voice had risen. Elijah's piercing blue eyes watched her intently but his face revealed nothing. "Sorry. It's been a long, busy day and—"

"You always get a tad snappy when you're hungry." Her father waved his hand. "Elijah, what do you think?"

Charity glanced back and forth at the two men. She had three more possible locations. Her father had already made up his mind. He just didn't want to admit he liked it. She knew her first choice would be a no. It had only been to throw the idea of having the gala in the hospital. Her father would have wanted to do that but it wouldn't be the success it could be. The cheesy suggestion would turn off any thought of having it there. The other possibilities were, well, possibilities. The diamond heritage would be very classy and right up her father's alley.

Elijah folded his hands on the table. His long fingers and smooth fingernails looked tanned against the white of the tablecloth. "As much as I would love to experience an American prom, I believe the Diamond place is more suitable for your birthday."

Charity smiled. "Agreed. What about you, Dad? I also have some other ideas."

The waitress arrived with their dinners and set their orders in front of them.

"In lieu of your snap turning into a roar, I settle for the Diamond thing as well." Her father set his napkin on his lap.

Inhaling the delicious aroma of roast chicken, Charity felt giddy. Possibly from the wine, the hunger, or getting her dad to agree to the location, she elbowed him lightly. "Wonder where I get that from?"

Chapter 6

They ate their meal with light conversation, Elijah and her dad doing most of the talking. They discussed hospital issues and a number of upcoming surgeries. A sense of wistful dreaming filled Charity. She had chosen to drop out of medical school and had absolutely no regrets, but that didn't mean she didn't miss it. For one millisecond she wondered if she had stayed, graduated and become a doctor, would she be sitting at this table talking with them about upcoming surgeries and post-op procedures?

She poured her second glass of wine of the evening and glanced around as she savoured her first sip. The lights had dimmed and the crowd had changed to a slightly younger generation. The bar was getting busy and the noise level had risen a few notches.

"... You two stay, finish the wine. I'll go and pay the bill."

Charity blinked and focused back on the conversation at the table. Her father stood and rested his fingers a slight moment on her shoulders as he stepped past her.

"Can you come by the hospital tomorrow or do you have an early return?"

She nodded. Her flight didn't leave until one p.m. "I can stop by. No problem. Thanks for dinner tonight."

"My pleasure. It was good to see you." He turned to Elijah. "You'll walk her to her car?" When Elijah nodded he added, "I'll see you at the hospital shortly."

She shifted in her seat so she could watch her father leave. He walked straight, smiled pleasantly at the hostess as he paid the bill, and disappeared out the door, never turning back to wave or glance at them. Her lips pressed tightly down. The next six months were going to be a challenge. How her mother stayed happily married to the man was beyond her understanding.

"What is it with the two of you?" Elijah's husky voice broke through her thoughts.

Darn that accent is sexy. He's gotta know it. Charity picked up her wine glass and took a sip. He'd probably prefer to talk about himself than the un-comings and lack of goings between her father and her. "You're from Australia, right?"

"New Zealand," he corrected.

"What made you decide to come to America?"

Elijah settled back in his chair. "Scholarship. Opportunity. And maybe just a little bit of running away from home."

"Running away?" *Interesting.*

"My mother's very much into the society club, the yacht club, and about any other club which exhibits social status. It seemed a good time to try something new."

Charity smiled teasingly. "Sounds pretty prestigious. I hardly doubt you needed a scholarship then."

Elijah grinned. "It fit the part back home and it looks good when you show up in med-school as a foreigner on scholarship. You earn a bit of respect before you start."

"Really?" She let her cheek rest against her hand and enjoyed the guilty pleasure of letting her elbow rest on the table. Her father would be cringing if he were still here. "I'd have thought it would've made you work harder to get the respect." She enjoyed another sip of wine and realized she'd almost finished this glass. She had better slow down or she wouldn't be driving home. She moved her head slightly so she could lean her chin against her palm. His backstory sounded interesting. "What made you want to be a doctor?"

It didn't seem possible, but Elijah's eyes lit up even more. "I had no idea what I wanted to do in high school." He shrugged. "I mean, if I asked my fifteen-year-old self what my plans where, I'd have said sports. I played varsity cricket in university so I started in kinesiology. My anatomy professor in first year talked me into being on the cadaver team. The team consisted of about ten students who cut open the Jane and John Does to teach the other students during class time. I was the only first year, and after ten minutes I knew it was where I wanted to be."

"Cutting up dead people?" She hoped her forced straight face wouldn't give her teasing away. "That's a bit serial psychopath sounding."

"Touché." He laughed. "It's weird, though, it just came naturally. All of it – the dissecting, the anatomy and physiology, like my brain knew it even though my subconscious did not."

"And you still enjoy it?"

"Every minute," he said without hesitation.

"That's very cool. Natural talent in medicine and surgery isn't easy to find. No wonder my father picked you as chief."

"Dr. Thompson is a great doctor. I'm honoured he hired me. When he said he was stepping down and wanted me to take over as chief, I'd be stupid to say no. This hospital is easily one of the top ten in the country. I get to do surgeries most hospitals would never risk and surgeons can only dream of. The other thing about Scott Thompson Hospital is the atmosphere. It's great. Everyone loves being here and that, in turn, helps the patients." He picked up his glass. "Sorry to ramble."

"Don't apologize. It's something you love."

He clinked his glass with hers. "Cheers to that." His elegant fingers rhythmically tapped against the rim of his glass. "I've been here five years now and don't recall seeing you around."

For three months straight, six years ago, I never left the place. That was before all the new construction and the renaming of the hospital to honour her father. "I've been by. You just probably never noticed me."

"I'd have definitely noticed."

She raised her eyebrows but didn't respond. *Was he flirting with her?*

"How long have you been raising money for hospitals?" He shot her an innocent look. "Not to sound clueless but... I have no clue what you do or how you can make a living out of it."

"There's money in this. Some for me, but the best part is that I get to spend other people's money to make more. I've been doing this about five or six years now. In America, Canada, and England. It's all about the money." She couldn't resist bantering him. "That's my job: raising money to pay for all these new wings you doctors want. So you guys can make loads and loads more money off those one-of-a-kind freaky surgeries."

He pointed a mocking finger at her. "This from the girl driving a Mustang."

"It's a rental! They gave it to me because they rented out all the cars from the size I reserved."

"Sure, that's what your cover story is." He chuckled, a husky, throaty one which sent little wrinkles by the sides of his eyes. It was very pleasant to watch and listen to.

"You're trouble."

"That depends..." His eyes locked with hers.

She enjoyed the last bit of her wine. "On what?"

He also took a sip of wine before answering. "On what kind of trouble you're looking for."

Charity watched him. Handsome, smooth, and so definitely a womanizer. He had probably already broken strings of hearts. Should she answer his question and open the doors to a chance of mischief? Did she need that right now? Did she want it? She did but not tonight. Flirting was a safe kind of fun. She had never done the one night stand thing and setting this gala up for her father meant she'd be back and forth here and constantly running into him at the hospital. Things between her father and her were awkward enough; she didn't need to add more to it. She pretended to check her watch.

"I should actually get back to the hospital." Elijah seemed to have read her thoughts and knew what to say. "I want to check my patients' charts from the past two hours. Plus I eventually need to get some sleep. I've had two nights on-call and another big surgery going on first thing in the morning."

"Ouch." She straightened and covered a yawn with her mouth. "Sorry. Been a busy week on my end also."

He helped her slip into her coat, his fingers accidentally brushing her neck. Her skin tingled on the spot where he had touched. Charity rubbed her scarf to try to erase or at least dampen the effect. She collected her briefcase and purse.

Elijah pointed to the half full bottle of white. "Almost a sin to leave unfinished."

"I won't tell anyone if you don't."

"Our little secret then?" He winked at her.

They walked to the exit, Elijah leading the way, and then holding the door for her. Outside they walked side by side. The brisk evening sent little puffs of air out of their mouths and noses. Charity was glad she'd brought her scarf. She stuffed her fingers deep inside her pockets.

"Where are you working now?" Elijah asked after a moment of comfortable silence.

"Atlanta. I just started a new contract this week."

"They don't mind you are working with another hospital at the same time?"

"I haven't mentioned anything because it's not a conflict of interest and I wasn't exactly sure what my father had in mind. It'll be a bit busy, but I can do most of the work here on weekends."

"So you'll be up here quite regularly then?"

She nodded. "I'll be up next weekend, and then probably two weeks after that I'll come up again. Whatever it takes to set it up."

"The Atlanta job, is it similar to this one?"

THE RECRUITING TRIP

"Not really. The contract we just signed is for two years. That hospital needs a new wing and a lot of expensive updates. It's not in bad enough shape to tear it down and start over but their other option—hiring me—figured out a way to get the place thriving again."

"It's interesting."

"Not really. My job is to basically find innovative ways to fundraise. To get people to want to give away a lot of money."

"Do you only work with hospitals?"

They turned a corner and a gust had Charity catching her breath. "Wow, it's windy. And to answer your question, right now I'm booked with just working with hospitals."

"So there's a queue to see you." He elbowed her lightly. "Why am I not surprised? How far are you booked ahead? Three months? Three years?"

She blushed despite the cold. He was flirting with her again. "Actually at the moment I don't have anything confirmed after Atlanta. Two years is a big commitment. Most places have their goal set for six months, maybe a year tops. I keep saying I'm going to take a break after I finish one project and before I jump into the next. It still hasn't happened. Maybe I'll finally go on a trip somewhere or a cruise or something." She stared ahead and didn't look at him. She couldn't believe she had just told him that she wanted a vacation. Could she sound any nerdier?

"I haven't been out of America for about five years now. I'm due for a holiday as well."

"You haven't gone home?"

"New Zealand? I planned on going last year but then got hired as chief so I didn't feel it was the right time to go."

They reached her car. "So you're a procrastinator as well?"

"I have my moments."

They both smiled and she fished around her purse for her keys. An awkward moment ensued when she didn't know what to say or do. Should she get in the car? Shake his hand? Hug him?

"Do you want a lift to the hospital?" She unlocked the doors using the key chain clicker.

He watched her, his gaze moving left to right like a slow pendulum intently staring into her eyes. "Tempting, but I should probably walk. Then I'll just catch the subway." He held out his hand. "I had a lovely time, Charity Thompson."

Tempting? Weird. It's just a ride. She reached out and shook his hand, part of her relieved, part of her extremely disappointed. "Me too. Have a nice evening, Dr. Bennett."

He waited for her to get into the car and start it before he began walking away.

This is the end of the Excerpt from
Saving Forever – Part 1

Saving Forever Series:

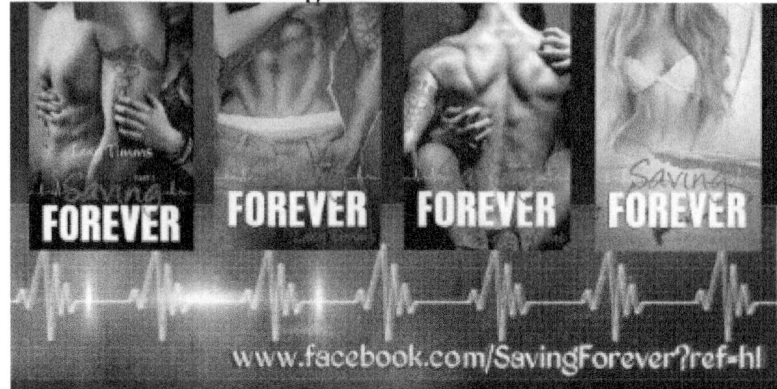

SAVING FOREVER SERIES
Book Trailer:
http://www.youtube.com/watch?v=ABs_uaeEamo
Website: https://www.facebook.com/SavingForever

THE RECRUITING TRIP   135

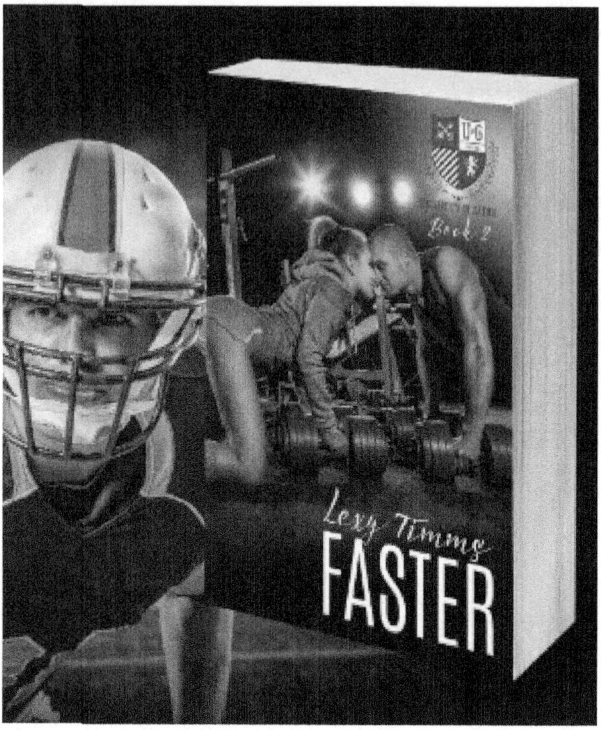
Book 2
Lexy Timms
FASTER

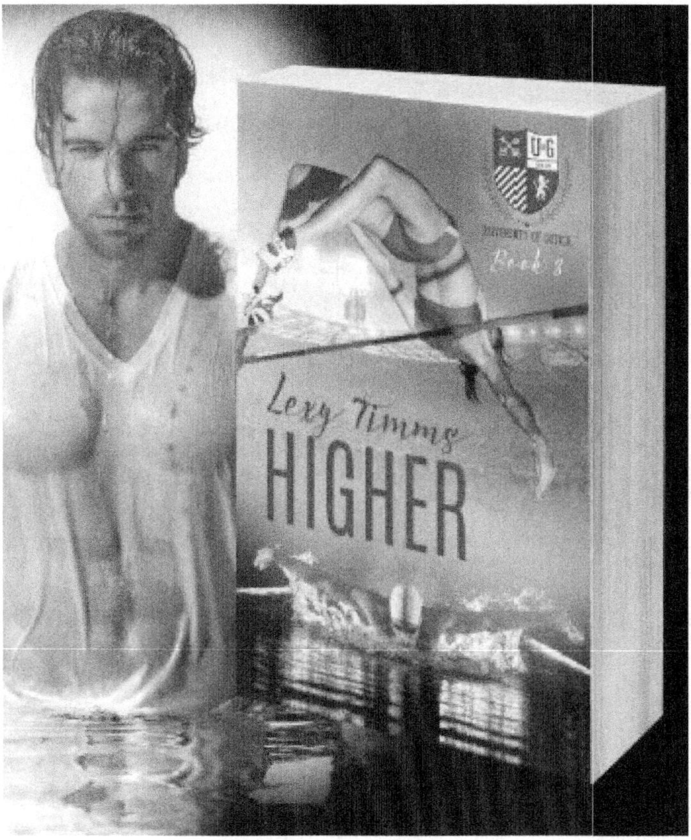
Lexy Timms
HIGHER
Book 8

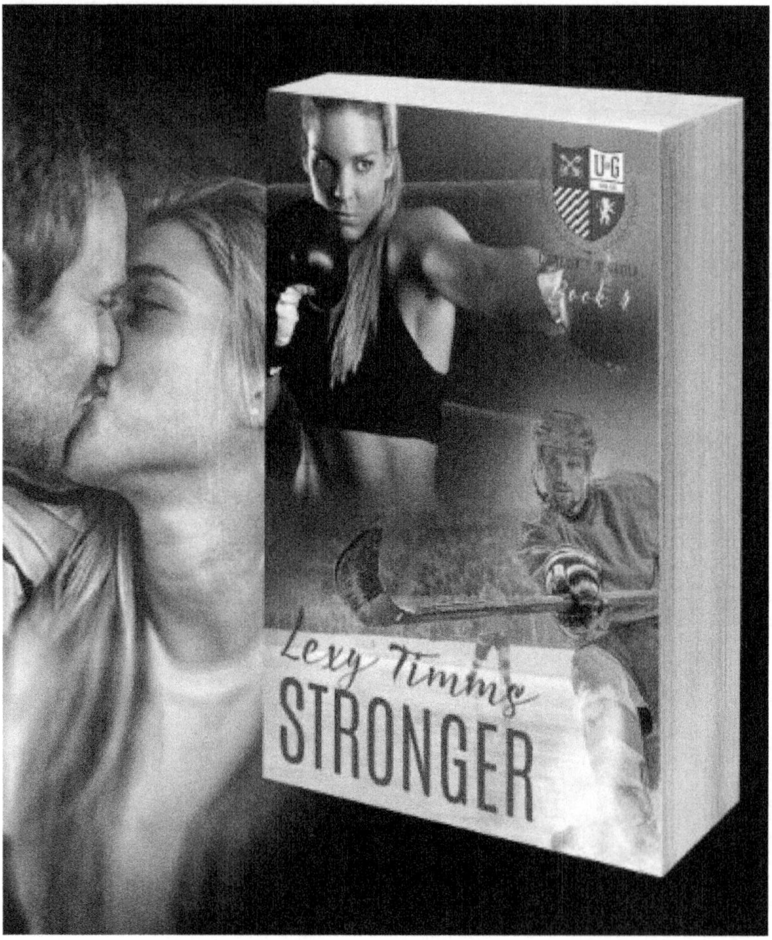
Lexy Timms
STRONGER

THE RECRUITING TRIP

THE RECRUITING Trip
Lexy Timms
THE RECRUITING Trip
Lexy Timms
Lexy Timms
THE RECRUITING
Trip

THE RECRUITING TRIP

UNIVERSITY OF GATICA

Did you love *The Recruiting Trip*? Then you should read *Saving Forever - Part 1* by Lexy Timms!

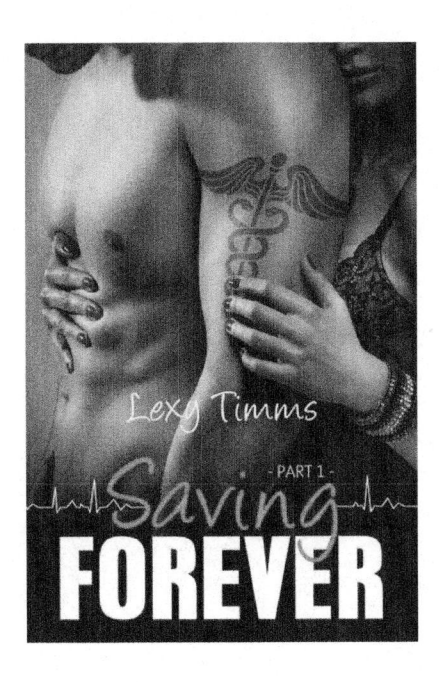

Charity Thompson wants to save the world, one hospital at a time. Instead of finishing med school to become a doctor, she chooses a different path and raises money for hospitals - new wings, equipment, whatever they need. Except there is one hospital she would be happy to never set foot in again--her fathers. So of course he hires her to plan a gala event for his sixty-fifth birthday. Charity can't say no. Now she is working in the one place she doesn't want to be. Except she's attracted to Dr. Elijah Bennet, the handsome playboy chief. Will she ever prove to her father that she's more than a med school dropout? Or will her attraction to Elijah keep her from repairing the one thing she desperately wants to fix? **this is NOT Erotica. It's a love story and romance that'll have you routing all the way for Charity***This is a FOUR book series, all your questions won't be answered in part 1*

Also by Lexy Timms

Saving Forever
Saving Forever - Part 1
Saving Forever - Part 2
Saving Forever - Part 3
Saving Forever - Part 4

The University of Gatica Series
The Recruiting Trip

Standalone
Wash
Loving Charity
Summer Lovin'
Christmas Magic: A Romance Anthology